Edge:
Ten Thousand Dollars, American

George G. Gilman

NEW ENGLISH LIBRARY
TIMES MIRROR

To P.H. for the true grit

An NEL Original
© by George G. Gilman 1971

*

FIRST NEL PAPERBACK EDITION FEBRUARY 1972
Reprinted May 1972
Reprinted July 1972
Reprinted January 1973
New Edition August 1973

*

NEL Books are published by
New English Library Limited from Barnard's Inn, Holborn, London, E.C.1.
Made and printed in Great Britain by Hunt Barnard Printing Ltd., Aylesbury, Bucks.

45001060 0

CHAPTER ONE

THE man lay in a prone position across the water-smoothed rocks of a dried up creek bed. He was dressed in a black shirt and black pants, sullied by sweat and the fine dust of southern Arizona Territory. His grey hat, dented at the crown, was a few inches from his outstretched right arm. His gunbelt held a full complement of charged cartridges, but the holster, tied to the thigh with a thong and the knife sheath at the back were empty. A slight bulge at the back of his neck where the shirt was stretched tight across his shoulders was a telltale of another weapon container which his attackers had not discovered.

He was a tall man, deceptively lean at first glance, for he carried a lot of weight which was evenly distributed – a great deal of it accounted for by well-developed muscles that made his clothes taut at the upper arms and thighs. Even as he was, unconscious and breathing raggedly, there was about this man an aura of the threat represented by his physical strength.

It was mid-morning of a fine summer day with the golden disc of the sun already high and cruel to everything on the sparse landscape that was not in shade. There was little sign of movement anywhere. Overhead, ugly black against the solid blue of the sky, three buzzards circled lazily, watching and waiting. To the south, just discernible through the water mirage of the heat, a cloud of dust marking the fast progress of a large group of riders. In the creek bed, the almost imperceptible rise and fall of the man's breathing. And, slithering across the trail that followed the course of the arid creek, a seven-foot long diamond-back rattler.

The man's first sign of returning awareness was a low groan to interrupt his regular breathing. Then a long-drawn out sigh, a convulsive jerk of his right leg from a cramp and he rolled over on to his back. He opened his eyes and snapped them shut again as strong sunlight stabbed into them. He lay still for several moments, lengthening his breathing rate, his face contorted in his fight against pain. It was a long, lean face with high cheekbones and a firm jawline. The mouth was thin-lipped, the eyes narrow with hooded lids. The skin, where it was visible above the stubble of a days' old beard was sun-baked to the colour and texture of well-tanned leather. The brow was made low by the fringe of straight black hair, which was worn long at the back and sides. It was the face of a man who seldom smiled: a face that some women found brutally attractive, others saw as ugly and men recognised as dangerous – the face of a cold-blooded killer.

The cause of the pain it showed was a large swelling beside the right eye, the skin discoloured to an ugly blue and black, split at the centre of the bruise so that blood had run, streaking the cheek and clotting to black among the stubble of the jaw. But the man was no stranger to pain and it took him only a few seconds to adjust from the emptiness of the unconscious to a state of awareness to his surroundings: a realisation that for the immediate future his mind would have to function against the pulsing throb of agony that engulfed the right side of his face.

He opened his eyes again, mere slits of light blue, the result of having a Scandinavian mother while almost everything else in the man's make-up was drawn from the pure blood Mexican heritage of his father. As he looked directly above, his lips drew back to show two rows of even white teeth in a cruel grin: high overhead the buzzards made a final circuit and wheeled away, screeching their frustrated rage.

'Stick with me, fellers,' he said softly after the departing scavengers. 'I'm as hungry for blood as you are.'

Then the grin was gone and if the buzzards had not lost interest they may have considered their wait worthwhile. For the man was at once unmoving to the extent that he suddenly filled his lungs with air and held it, his chest expanding and the veins of his neck standing out with the effort. The slithering sound of the snake's length as it hauled itself down into the creek bed and the periodic rattle from its swaying tail were magnified by the silence.

6

EDGE:
TEN THOUSAND DOLLARS,
AMERICAN

Without moving his head, the man swivelled his eyes to the right to their full extent, looked along the rocky bed and saw the diamond-back approaching. The snake seemed unaware of the man stretched across its path, saw him merely as a low obstacle to its progress. If it did see glistening beads of sweat ooze from wide open pores and form into rivulets to cut irregular courses across dust streaked flesh, it chose to ignore them. It moved at a regular, unhurried pace, muscles expanding and contracting to inch its thick length across the broken surface, cold eyes blinking, forked tongue flicking out through half-opened jaws in which its venomous fangs glinted.

The man, his muscles aching with the strain of their enforced quiescence, his crowded lungs gaining only slight relief as he allowed stale air to trickle out through his nostrils, watched the snake without fear but with a deep respect for the reptile's ability to kill him.

The diamond-back had reached him now, raised its head to survey the extent of the obstruction. The man watched the tiny eyes, could sense the working of the reptilian brain which decided after several moments of thought that it was easier to slither up and over rather than by-pass the obstacle. The decision taken, the snake chose a course across the man's chest and his eyes swiveled in their sockets, watching the head, fighting an urge to blink as saline sweat spread over the irises. The dry warmth of the reptile's body penetrated the man's shirt, threatening to cause an involuntary quiver of his flesh. Then the snake's head found the rocks on the other side of the man and the animal seemed anxious to get clear, began to drag itself along at a faster rate, the frequency of the tail rattle increasing.

The man allowed his pent up breath to escape more rapidly, felt the first tremor of dizziness just as the snake slithered clear of him. He remained immobile a moment longer, sucked a great gust of clean air into his aching lungs and sprang to his feet, ignoring the needles of pain that jabbed his face. The rattler heard and saw the movement, and its head came up and turned, mouth gaping, fangs glistening. Instinctively the man's hand went for a gun, his face twisting into silent rage as he found the holster empty. His left hand tried for the knife at the small of his back and the vacant sheath raised a roar of frustration to his throat. The rattler began to coil the length of its body, head swaying, tongue flicking, eyes unblinking.

It was as fearless as the man, with its own brand of animal respect for threatened danger. Then there was a blur of motion, the man crouching to snatch up a rock with his left hand as his right streaked to the back of his neck. The rock left his hand with enormous force, smashing into the coil of body, causing the diamond-back to writhe in agony. Then the man was out of the crouch, leaping forward with feet together, the heels of his boots landing with a terrific impact upon the snake's neck. Then, as the reptile struggled to twist, to strike at vulnerable flesh, the man's right hand swung down, the blade of an open razor sliding from the finger tips. The edge, keened to a perfect sharpness, sliced through the neck of the snake with hardly a slowing of its momentum to indicate it had passed through solid matter. The headless body of the reptile gave one convulsive jerk of dying tissue and was still.

The man, who had been born with a full name but who was now called 'Edge' stood for several seconds on the dead body of the diamond-back, then wiped the blade of the razor clean of blood on his pants' leg before returning it to the neck pouch. Then he looked around him, eyes narrowed against the hard brightness of the sun, rested upon a deep patch of shadow thrown by a large boulder. As he finally moved, dragging heavy feet, towards the shade, the sunlight glinted on the tin star pinned to his shirt front.

He eased his tense, aching body to the ground and sighed, his features set into a hard expression of bitter pensiveness as he recalled the events of the morning.

CHAPTER TWO

PEACEVILLE, Arizona Territory had lived up to its new name
during the four weeks in which the man called Edge had been
temporary sheriff. As the days went lazily by, the physical and
mental wounds Edge had suffered in avenging the death of his
brother had healed.* He spent his days either behind the desk in
the sheriff's office or patrolling the two streets that formed the
town. He spoke little to anyone and his demeanour was such
that few were moved to open conversations with him. He ate
regularly, three square meals a day, at the restaurant owned by
the Mexican nicknamed Honey and the only relationship he
had with anybody in depth involved Gail, the beautiful waitress who tended tables at the restaurant. She it was who became
a willing receptacle for his infrequent bouts of sexual passion.
It was her softly firm body, large-breasted, narrow-waisted
and strongly-hipped that suffered the savage onslaught of his
hard maleness: submitting with the compliance of a deeply
eager love to a man she knew to be devoid of emotion.

For Edge was a man who only took and never gave.

He was as content as such a man could ever be; eating,
sleeping, loving and getting paid three dollars a day for work
that was never more demanding than a simple nightly task of
arresting the town drunk and throwing him into one of three
cells at the rear of the sheriff's office. Until El Matador and
his group of twenty bandits crossed the border from the Mexican province of Sonora and blew a hole in the rear safe of
Norman Chase's bank.

They came at dawn, riding at a gallop until they sighted the
town, its buildings rising up off the desert floor to provide a
man-made scar on the desolate landscape. They were all big
men, except one. Dressed in white pants and shirts, criss-

* See: *Edge : The Loner*. (New English Library.)

crossed by heavily-laden bandoliers, with moustachioed faces shaded by large sombreros, they rode with rifles carried in hands and many sported naked swords slid through waist-bands. The small man was the leader, El Matador – The Killer. He was no more than five feet tall, with a stocky build that hinted at a wiry strength without advertising aggression. But his young face – he was not yet twenty-five – mirrored the events of a crowded and violent youth that had earned him his *nom de guerre*. It was a face of undisguised evil, evident in the widely-set eyes and twisted mouth, the firm jawline scarred by a diagonal knife wound and the overall set of the features aged into a permanent expression of hate for everything and every-body.

He rode a magnificent white stallion at the head of the column of men and was dressed like the others. But his weapons were different. He carried a Turkish-made blunderbuss with a rosewood stock beautifully inlaid with silver and in holsters at each hip were slung twin American Colt Army Model revolvers.

As soon as he saw the buildings of Peaceville take form in the grey light of dawn he raised a hand and his men obediently slowed their horses to the pace set by the white stallion. Miguel, who was an enormously fat man with bulbous cheeks and a gold ring in his right ear, and acted as El Matador's lieutenant, cantered forward from the column to ride beside his leader.

'How much you think is in the Peaceville bank?' he asked in Spanish.

Matador drew in his cheeks and sucked upon them for a few moments, staring ahead. 'A great deal,' he replied at length. 'The gringos in Washington offer much money to bounty hunters who capture outlaws. The hunters demand quick pay-ment. They will not wait. Much money will be there.'

Miguel laughed raucously. 'But it will not be bounty hunters who get it, El Matador.'

The bandit leader seldom laughed and when Miguel recog-nised upon the evil face an expression which indicated El Matador was thinking, he reined in his own horse, dropped back to his position in the line. When the group were within a quarter mile of the town their leader signalled they should dismount and the men did so, listened attentively to the instructions they were given. Then they split into three groups, two of nine and one of three: the smallest comprised Matador, Miguel and an older, pock-marked man named Torres. One of the large groups moved off first, leading their horses at a steady run in a wide circle that would take them to the other side of Peaceville. When they had almost reached their position, the trio set off in a direct line for town and as soon as they were seen to reach the wall of the first building the second large group closed in.

The sun had not yet showed itself over the mountain range far in the east and no citizen of Peaceville was even close to stirring in preparation for the new day. The only living thing which moved on the street was a large white dog, which growled a token threat and then returned to its scavenging as the trio of Mexican bandits ducked into the alley beside the bank, whispering softly to their horses to prevent them being spooked by the surrounding silence. In the alley, Miguel handed the reins of his mount to Matador, then took up a position from which he could survey the street, his Colt Revolving rifle cocked and ready.

Behind the bank building, Matador led all three horses towards a tall cactus and hitched the reins over a side shoot. Then he watched with glinting eyes as Torres moved towards the bank wall, drawing a large pouch from under his shirt. He placed this at the foot of the adobe wall, grunted and moved it a few inches to the left. Then he stood and backed away, began to whisper quietly to the horses. Matador nodded to him and withdrew one of the Colts, pursed his lips to emit a low whistle. Down at the mouth of the alley Miguel raised his free hand to signal that the men were in position.

Matador crouched and fired and the powder-filled pouch exploded with a roar, sending flames and dense smoke skywards, tearing great chunks of adobe from the wall. The horses panicked, but were held fast by the cactus as Matador and Torres moved through the reeking smoke, began tearing aside loose masonry to enlarge the hole. Out on the street hoofbeats began to resound between the façades of buildings as the two groups of riders galloped into town from each end, firing with-

11

out aiming at windows and doors as the rudely awakened citizens scrambled from their beds.

One bullet smashed through a cabin window and imbedded itself harmlessly into the dirt floor but a shard of flying glass skimmed across the room, buried its pointed end into the side of a man's neck, severing an artery and drawing a gush of blood. A whore threw open a window on the second floor of the Rocky Mountain Saloon and as she craned out to see what was happening had the whole left side of her face blown away as a heavy calibre shell tore into the flesh. Her naked body fell through the window, bounced off the roof of the sidewalk below and landed on the street to be trampled by galloping hoofs. Norman Chase, who had been rocked from sleep with the certain knowledge that his bank was the source of the explosion, rushed from the New York Hotel in his nightshirt, firing wildly with a pepper-box, screaming abuse at the invaders. A laughing bandit, shirt wide open to reveal a heavily scarred chest steered his horse into a wide turn, drawing his ivory hilted sword. The blade flashed in the first rays of the morning sun and sliced off the crown of Chase's head like a knife peeling an apple.

Edge came awake with the roar of the exploding powder, hand going instinctively to the twelve shot Henry repeater rifle beneath the bunk in the open cell at the back of the sheriff's office. But before he was halfway across the office feet thudded on to the sidewalk outside as two bandits leapt from their horses. The door was kicked open and two shots whined through the gap, clanged against the cell bars. Edge dived for the floor as the town drunk died with a ricochet burning a course through his open mouth and into his brain.

'We will kill you if you so much as blink an eyelid, señor,' a flat voice said in accented English.

Edge stayed flat against the floor. 'My nose itches,' he said, against the racket of gunfire from the street, punctuated by the death scream of Norman Chase.

'Scratch and you won't itch nowhere no more,' came the reply, and the footfalls came into the office.

Three dollars a day wasn't worth dying for, so Edge did not move as the men approached him, one taking the Henry from

12

his hand, the other lowering a rifle muzzle to nudge him behind the left ear. It was hot from firing and singed Edge's neck hair.

'Get up slow, señor,' he was told. 'Like you were in a tub of black treacle.'

Edge did so, heard a grunt and felt the knife snatched from its sheath at the back of his belt. Edge only removed his clothes and weapons when he took a bath or made love. He looked into the grinning face of each Mexican, saw in their dark eyes the enjoyment they were deriving from the violence and their triumph. They were hopeful he would make a play. One of them took a cigarillo from behind his ear, ignited it: took a fresh one and lodged it in the resting place vacated by the first.

'We are robbing the bank,' the other one said in a conversational tone as the shooting died down outside, finally ended.

'Never did trust those places,' Edge said. 'Bankers ain't going to do much to protect other people's money.'

'You're the law, you should protect the bank,' the man with the cigarillo pointed out.

'How many are you?' Edge asked.

'Twenty, led by El Matador.'

Edge grinned coldly. 'I figure the money's yours,' he said.

They both grinned. 'I think this is a wise man, Juan,' one said.

'Wise men live longer,' replied the second.

'But not very much longer.'

They both laughed. Then, while the smoker leaned his rump against the desk and kept his rifle trained steadily upon Edge's chest, the other started to search the office, opening drawers and cupboards and spilling their contents haphazardly across the floor. With each discovery of what was to him worthless rubbish, his expression darkened. Even after he had found the key to the safe his mood did not return to its former humour. For there was only a half-empty bottle of whiskey inside and when he had taken a long pull at it, was no nearer finding any money.

So he ceased the search and came to stand directly in front of Edge. He was shorter than the big, lean man, but his fellow

bandit's rifle more than compensated this physical disadvantage.

'You don't trust banks, señor,' he said softly, hardly moving
his lips. 'So where you keep your money?'

Edge treated him to a mean grin. 'I'm a lawman,' he said.
'Not a bandit. I don't have any money.'

The Mexican's hand lashed out and the back of it thudded
into Edge's face. Edge did not so much as blink an eye.

'Not so wise, señor. I think you are going to die. Maybe it
could be easy, or maybe hard. You get wise again, and we
make it easy.' He reached up a grimed finger and prodded
Edge just above the ear. 'Here a bullet is good. Here, not so
good.' He jabbed Edge with a short, powerful fist into the
lower belly.

Escaping air whooshed out of Edge's mouth, but he made
no other sound. The Mexican rubbed his knuckles, bruised by
the hard ridge of stomach muscles. The other bandit, while he
kept the rifle levelled, allowed his gaze to wander about the
office and his face was suddenly wreathed by a grin again as
his eyes fastened upon a loose board high on one wall.

'Juan,' he called softly.

The other looked at him with irritation, saw him motion
with the cigarillo towards the board.

'What you think?'

Juan snapped his attention back to Edge, caught a sudden
angry narrowing of the slit eyes.

'I think we found it,' Juan said and moved quickly, dragging
a chair across the floor and climbing on to it. He tore aside the
board and gave a yell of delight as he saw the bills stacked on
a joist. 'Such a rich lawman,' he said, clawing the money from
its hiding place. 'I think when I retire from being a bandit I
become sheriff in a gringo town.'

Even two thousand five hundred wasn't worth dying for in
Edge's book. But Jamie had died for two thousand of it, and the
death of his kid brother put the matter in a different light. Not
to die for. But to take the risk. At a time when the risk was
worth taking.

'What are you doing in there?'

The voice came from the now quiet street, authoritative,

14

speaking the kind of Spanish Edge had learned from his father.

'We found the sheriff had a bank of his own,' Juan shouted in reply.

'Outside.'

The smoker dropped his cigarillo and mashed it beneath his boot, jabbed the rifle muzzle viciously into Edge's side.

'You heard what El Matador said,' he commanded. 'Move.'

'And I guess he ain't talking bull,' Edge answered, and moved.

CHAPTER THREE

THE bandits were formed into a half circle of defence across the front of the sheriff's office, menacing an otherwise empty street. The dead Norman Chase was inside the defences, the trampled saloon whore outside. Also inside was El Matador and Torres each with a bulging canvas sack at his feet. Edge, emerging in front of the guns of the two men who had disarmed him took in the scene at a glance, had to do a double take at the bandit leader to check that he was not a child, so small was he. But he saw in the dark brown face a kinship with the set of his own features and he knew this was a man who had lived with violence.

Matador also sensed an affinity and he seemed to find it confusing. His dark eyes fastened on the face of Edge for a short moment, flicked to Juan.

'How much you find?' he demanded.

Edge looked over the heads of the half circle of bandits, searching for a sign of retaliation from the town. He did not expect it, but one had to take account of the unexpected. At the first sign of trouble the sheriff would be blasted, so Edge figured he had to anticipate the moves if he wanted a chance of survival.

'Many hundreds of dollars,' Juan said with pride, pulling a handful of samples from inside his shirt. 'Maybe thousands.'

The exchange had been in Spanish. Now Matador looked at Edge with a kind of respect, and spoke English.

'You are a crooked lawman?' he asked.

'I am not a lawman,' Edge replied in Spanish, his knowledge of the language providing the bandit leader with another jolt of surprise. 'Somebody killed the real sheriff. I killed the killer. The town gave me a job.'

'At such a salary?' In Spanish.

'No.'

Matador did not like the single negative. Then he shrugged. 'No matter. We do not care where the money comes from. Just so long as it comes to us. Dinero has no allegiance.'

Edge did not answer, and Matador didn't like this, either. He leaned forward to open the mouth of the sack and indicated that Juan should bring his find and deposit it with the money from the bank. As he did so, several of the bandits on guard duty shuffled their feet restlessly and licked their lips, greedy eyes watching the bills fall into the sack. Others paid no attention, but maintained their concentration on the street. It was too quiet: there was hanging over the town the kind of silence that portends danger and the more sensitive members of the band could feel this and it made them nervous. Edge watched the money going into the sack: old, loose bills that fluttered in the still, morning air. Juan stepped back with a finality of movement, grinning and waiting expectantly for a word of praise. Matador merely waved him away as he pulled the cord to close the mouth of the sack. Edge ran his eyes over the figure of Juan, trying to spot where he had concealed the solid block of five hundred dollars which had been his bounty for killing his brother's murderers. He decided it had to be in the folds of his loose fitting shirt.

Matador turned his back upon Edge and looked to left and right along the street, between the ring of bandits. His voice was loud, his English heavily accented, but good.

'You people got nothing to gain from causing us trouble,' he shouted. 'We're leaving now 'cause we got what we came for. We take your sheriff and anyone shoots, we blast him to hell. Then we set fire to every building in this town and we take every woman who don't look like a horse. We rape them, then we slice them up. You figure out if that's worth the lives of a few lousy Mexican bandits.'

Several bandits who understood English laughed, perhaps to prove to themselves they were unmoved by their leader's easy insult.

'Bring the horses,' Matador called in Spanish and two of the band came from the rear of the Rocky Mountain Saloon, leading the mounts of the rest. The men mounted in small groups, so that there was always a number of guns primed for trouble.

There was no horse for Edge. Torres swung astride his mount, hefting the sack in front of him. Then Matador.

'Out to the head of the line,' the leader instructed, drawing and waving a Colt.

Edge sighed and stepped down off the sidewalk, went to the centre of the street and halted, looked over his shoulder to see his personal guard mount. Matador holstered his revolver and pointed the foreign scatter gun.

'Now you walk, lawman,' the leader commanded. 'This gun is not new, but it has lost none of its power. Anybody else who tries to stop us, I will blow off your head with it. If you attempt to escape, I will aim lower and death will be much slower. Move.'

Edge began to walk and Matador allowed him a space of ten yards before urging his horse forward. His men followed as a group behind him, eyes roving the buildings on each side, glancing ahead and back. It might have been a ghost town. In front, nothing. Behind, the settling dust raised by the many hoofs: until a shape broke from cover and the bandit at the end of the line raised his rifle, finger shaking so much he missed the trigger. Then a nervous giggle erupted from his lips as he saw the big white dog dash across the street.

CRACK.

The shot seemed to tremble the air over the whole town and Edge tensed his entire body for the stinging impact of whatever was loaded into Matador's blunderbuss. But no bandit had fallen and they did not break stride as they glanced back down the street. The big white dog lay on its side, its snout still buried into the bloody pulp inside the opened skull of Norman Chase. A wisp of smoke rose from an open second-storey window of the hotel.

'I thought Americans loved dogs,' Matador said. 'You live a little longer, señor.'

When they had ridden clear of the town by some two hundred yards, Matador called a halt. Edge turned to face the band.

'You ride now,' the leader told Edge.

'Why we not killed him here,' Juan said. 'They will not come after us.'

Matador's eyes narrowed. 'Who is your leader?' he asked softly and Juan's expression became sullen under the steady stare.

'You are, El Matador,' he answered, hanging his head.

Matador nodded, looked at Edge and pointed to Juan. 'You ride with him. Here, beside me.'

Juan heeled his mount forward, halted her so that Edge could swing up behind him. Matador raised his hand and the band moved off again, heading south in no haste. One of the men at the back began to whistle tunelessly. Edge rode with his arms wrapped around the waist of the man in the saddle, but kept his face averted, diminishing the effect of Juan's rancid smell.

'Where did you learn to speak our language?' Matador asked suddenly after they had rode in silence for some time.

'From my father,' Edge answered, annoyed that his line of thought had been interrupted. He had been watching Matador, noting the casual way he carried the Turkish gun, the looseness of the Colt in the holster on his side. He thought he could slit Juan's throat, grab the two guns and blast Matador from the saddle: maybe take two other men with the Colt before he went down under a hail of bullets. There was no chance for survival, of course. But, perhaps in another plan, his life was not so worthless. Just one bandit would die now. Edge decided he had the patience to wait his time for the rest.

'You speak it well,' Matador said in a conversational tone. 'Your father was a good teacher of the language.'

'He spoke it like a native,' Edge replied.

Matador looked deep and long at Edge as they jogged along. Then he nodded. 'You have the look of Mexico in your face, señor . . . what is your name?'

'They call me Edge.'

'Your father was Mexican?'

Edge nodded.

'Not your mother?'

'No.'

'You do not have a Mexican name.'

'It's a long story.'

Matador raised his hand and reined in his horse. They had reached a point on the trail south where a dried-up creek bed curved in from the west.

'It is a pity you do not have the time to tell it,' Matador said, glancing back over his shoulder. The horizon was shrouded in a heat mirage which cloaked Peaceville as effectively as a heavy mist. His eyes fastened back upon Edge's face. 'I think you understand why I cannot let you live,' he said and Edge thought he detected a note of apology in the voice. He decided it had to be Matador's brand of humour.

'Your men wouldn't like it,' Edge said as Juan tried to break the grip around his waist, anxious to get clear of the agony that was to blast in a wide angle from the evil-looking blunderbuss.

Matador made a deep-throated sound of disgust. 'I do not consult this scum when I make a decision,' he said and glowered back at his men to see the effect of this new insult. To a man they grinned at him in a collective parody of good humour. 'They represent no threat to me,' he said, turning his attention to Edge. 'But you, señor Edge.' He drew in his breath. 'You are different. I see in your face a look I could fear if I understood what fear was. I let you live and I think I would spend much time looking over my shoulder.'

'That bothers you?' Edge asked evenly, getting a forceful whiff of evil origin as fresh sweat broke from Juan to reactivate the staleness of the old.

Matador shook his head. 'No, it does not bother me. Except that one time I might not look over my shoulder. And you are a man who would not shrink from shooting an enemy in the back.'

'It's safer that way,' Edge said as the blunderbuss was raised and levelled. 'Maybe I could buy my life.'

Matador halted his movement, narrowed eyes showing bewilderment mingled with suspicion. 'We have already taken your money.'

'Not all of it,' Edge said, maintaining his vice-like grip on the trembling Juan.

'How much more you got?'

20

Edge pursed his lips. 'Five hundred dollars. Maybe a few loose bills.'

'Where?'

Edge suddenly released his grip and streaked a hand inside Juan's shirt, popping buttons. The bandit released a sound of horror as the hand came out holding the block of money. Throughout the ride it had been held pressed against Juan's sweating side by Edge's forearm. It smelled of the man.

'Here,' Edge said.

Matador's cruel eyes flashed from the money to the face of Juan. Every muscle in the bandit's body was trembling and his mouth worked soundlessly for several moments as he struggled to hold his leader's withering gaze.

'I did not know,' he managed to gasp finally. 'El Matador, please. As soon as I found it hiding in my clothes I would have given it to you.'

'Give it to me now,' Matador demanded, his voice as hard as the rosewood stock he gripped.

Sobbing, Juan snatched the block of dollars from Edge's hand and reached out towards his leader. Edge looked on without breathing, his eyes narrowed to the merest slits, knowing that a miscalculation by a split second could end his life. Chances were he would die anyway, but self-preservation is an instinct that refused to accept defeat.

At the moment he saw Matador's finger whiten at the knuckle curled around the trigger, Edge pushed himself backwards, his seat sliding over the hind-quarters of Juan's horse. He heard the gun explode into thunderous sound and felt a searing pain beside his right eye before the sun went out and empty darkness enfolded him. He did not know that a piece of ball shot had smashed into his face, causing a gush of blood: he did not feel his limp body thud into the ground at the edge of the trail and slide down to become an inert, face-down shape in the stream bed.

Neither did he see Juan catch the full blast of the blunderbuss load on the side of his head; the great shower of blood, mangled flesh and shattered bone; the horse bolts forward with its dead rider still mounted, head hanging at a crazy angle and attached to the body by a few strands of lifeless tissue.

21

Nor the block of bills as it sailed up into the air with a death spasm of a hand, to be neatly caught by the impassive, pock-marked Torres, who thrust the money into his sack.

Matador looked from the bolting horse to Edge, his eyes showing satisfaction. He patted the elaborately decorated stock of his weapon.

'I think maybe I killed two birds with one stone as the gringos say,' he muttered in English. 'One a jackdaw and one an eagle.' He raised his hand. 'We ride.'

This last in Mexican. They went at the gallop.

CHAPTER FOUR

EDGE accepted the facts of what had happened to him that morning without experiencing anger. As he raised himself from out of the shade of the boulder and started back down the trail towards Peaceville, his face was a mask of cold emptiness, blank of any expression. His mind was laid as waste as his features for there was nothing with which it could work. El Matador had robbed him and El Matador was a Mexican who would ride south across the border. The decision was made. He needed his horse, his guns and his knife and Edge would go south.

The town was still in a state of shock from the violence of its early morning waking. Its citizens went about their normal business with the unhurried movements of people in a daze. Physical signs of the bandit raid were in the process of being erased as a group of men worked at repairing the hole in the rear of the bank, householders and businessmen fixed broken windows and, in the church the priest tolled the death knell as two gravediggers sweated outside.

As Edge started down the street, heading for the sheriff's office, he became the object of shocked recognition which quickly transformed into expressions of mute accusation. He should have been dead: that he was not indicated a sell-out. And men like El Matador did not enter into deals without strong reasons.

Edge ignored the looks and the people. They owed him nothing and he felt not a flicker of interest in them. They had used each other for as long as it suited all parties and now that was over.

'Edge!'

He recognised the voice and knew he was passing Honey's Restaurant, glanced over to the door showing no sign of halting his steady pace. Gail, the paleness of her complexion and residue of horror in her eyes not detracting from her beauty, beckoned to him from the doorway.

'Edge!' she said again, on a rising pitch when she saw he was ignoring her. 'You're walking into a trap.'

This brought him up abruptly. He took a final look ahead down the street, narrowed eyes searching for danger, then stared at the girl.

'You part of it?'

'There's two territorial marshals in your office,' she said.

Edge looked round again, obliquely at the front of the sheriff's office. He saw no movement there and crossed quickly to step up on to the sidewalk, brush into the restaurant as Gail stood back. The tables were empty, set for breakfast on a day when nobody had felt like eating.

'Lunchtime will be slow as well,' Edge said, looking towards the door to the kitchen. 'Where's your boss?'

'Honey's fixing the funeral arrangements. They killed three people, Edge.'

She closed the door, looked with concern at the man's facial injury.

'Tell me about the lawmen,' he demanded.

'You're hurt.' She approached him. 'Come into the kitchen. I'll clean it before it becomes infected.'

Edge's arm came up and he hit her back-handed across the cheek.

'The lawmen!' he demanded harshly as Gail's eyes filled with the tears of pain and she raised a delicate hand to her face. But in the next moment those same eyes spat hate at him. The kind of hate that is just over the dividing line from love.

'You can't hurt me,' she threw at him. 'You can beat me to a pulp and you'll still be the only man I'll ever love. And I'm not going to help you get clear of Peaceville only to have you die with a body full of gangrene.' The fire died in her eyes and her voice softened. 'Now, get into the kitchen, you big oaf.'

Edge's hands clenched into hard-knuckled fists and his cold eyes bore into those of the girl. Then he suddenly spun and went between the tables, knocking over chairs as he cut a direct route through to the kitchen door. Gail followed him, a tiny smile playing at the corners of her mouth, which she wiped away as he sat down at a table and his eyes found her again. She had learned just how far she could push this man of iron in whose make-up a pinprick of regard for her provided the only vulnerable spot.

A pot of water was already near the boil on the large, wood-fired stove and she poured some into an iron basin, and got a length of clean cloth from a drawer.

'They rode in an hour ago,' she said as she pressed the hot, soaking cloth against Edge's wound, angry at herself for feeling a stab of satisfaction when he winced. 'They've got a wanted poster on somebody called Josiah Hedges. Captain Josiah C. Hedges. Picture looks like you a lot younger. Hedges ... Edge. A man you killed called you Captain. Close enough?'

'Not so younger,' Edge allowed. 'Close enough. It wasn't murder.'

'The authorities don't rate it very highly,' Gail said, pouring the reddened water away, getting some fresh and beginning to clean up where the blood had matted into his beard. 'They've put a bounty on you. Only a hundred dollars.'

Edge turned on his grin of ice. 'Even I wouldn't kill me to raise just that much. How'd you know all this?'

'I thought you might be back,' she answered evenly, with a toss of her long hair. 'Didn't want anyone to steal your belongings. I went to the office to get them. The marshals came while I was there. Asked me what had happened. I told them and then they showed me the wanted poster, wanted to know if I had seen the man called Hedges.'

'Obliged,' Edge said, getting to his feet as she finished cleaning his face. 'Where's my gear?'

'Out back,' she said, nodding to the door. 'There's a horse out there, as well. It's mine. Fed, watered, saddled and ready to go.' She licked her lips and reached out a hand to touch his shoulder as he turned. 'Edge?'

'Yeah?'

'I'm not going to ask to come with you. But if you ask me it won't take long to saddle Honey's horse.'

'Where I'm going, women ain't nothing but something to screw,' he said harshly, saw her wince. His voice softened and

25

he leaned forward, brushed his lips gentle across her mouth. 'You're a good screw, Gail, but you got other qualities.'

Tears welled into her eyes again, and her hand found his, pressed some crumpled bills into the palm.

'Twelve dollars,' she whispered. 'It's all I have.'

'I'll repay it through the mail,' he told her and strode to the door.

'You won't be coming back?'

He looked at her with hooded eyes. 'What for?'

'I . . . I guess nothing.'

'Nothing ain't worth coming back for,' he said and went out.

The door slammed and she heard the sound of him mounting. The horse whinneyed and then hoofs thudded into a gallop. Gail sat down on the still warm chair and threw her head on to the table, gave herself up to sobs that sent tremors through her entire body.

Honey and the two hard-faced marshals found her like that.

CHAPTER FIVE

EDGE had no idea how far it was to the Mexican-Arizona territory border. He just knew it was south and that was the way he rode, keeping the high, hot sun ahead of him when the trail petered out. It was desolate country, arid and irregularly featured by high outcrops of rock, dry stream beds and grotesquely shaped cactus plants. It seemed upon first impression to be a dead place, for even the giant prickly growths and infrequent patches of sharp-edged grass seemed to be formed of rock, so still were they in the unmoving air. But Edge and his horse were not the only living things that moved in the area of vast waste through which they passed.

When Edge was well clear of town and slowed the horse to conserve her energy he had time to look about him. He saw a diamond-back rattler almost as big as the one he killed that morning, coiled in the shade of a rock, a beautifully patterned copperhead on the move, and a bizarrely decorated gila monster which darted across his path, causing his horse to rear up.

But he soothed her into docility again and she fell back into her even gait, obediently responding to a tug on the reins that headed her towards a small canyon that split asunder the high solid face of a stretch of plateau country that stretched across the horizon. As he neared the canyon mouth, Edge saw that a wide slash of disturbed dust curved in from the west. As further evidence of the passage of a great many horses, dried dung sprinkled the ground. Edge could see how the riders had been heading directly into the sheer face of the towering cliffs, had made a broad, wheeling turn to go into the canyon which provided the only route south for many miles on either side.

'I figure my money came this way,' Edge muttered and the horse pricked up her ears. The rider leaned forward and ruffled the short, tough hair between them. Then, when he heeled her into a gallop, she seemed to be as anxious as the man to reach the shade afforded by the canyon. It was mid-afternoon now and the sun, as hot as ever, was slanting its light and heat from the west, so that the western wall of the canyon threw a giant shadow. But not for any great distance, for although the canyon was narrow at its opening, it broadened almost at once, the boulder littered ground on each side sloping away fast like the sides of a shallow bowl. Ahead was an expanse of desert country as desolate as the plain Edge had just crossed, but featured with many more outcrops and sparsely vegetated hills.

Edge stayed in the shade for as long as he could see the tracks made by the Mexicans' horses. But they were on the far side of the canyon, the Mexicans having taken advantage of the shadow of the eastern wall thrown out by morning sunlight. And soon he was forced out into the harsh glare again in order to keep on the trail of his quarry.

His horse died beneath him while still on all fours, the sound she made as she collapsed, throwing him clear, merely the whoosh of air venting from crushed lungs. The rifle crack that had sent a bullet piercing into her brain echoed between the canyon walls with such stark clarity that the sound stung Edge's ears. He lay absolutely still where he had fallen, shielded on one side by the bulk of the dead horse, exposed on the other where there was just an expanse of open terrain scattered with small rocks.

It was from this side that the two men approached and Edge did not have to move in his bogus unconsciousness to watch them, for he had landed on his belly, head on the side and facing that way. He watched them with eyes cracked open the merest extent, seeing them through the dark curtain of his lashes. The sharp-shooter had been good or lucky. It had been a long-range, downwards shot from two hundred yards away, a hundred feet above the canyon floor. He saw them appear from each side of a huge boulder, stand for a moment looking down at him, then start forward. Even winded as he was, his head still ringing with the sound of the shot and the thud of his body on to the hard ground, Edge knew he could gun them both down in less than two seconds – if the Henry repeater was in his hands. But the rifle was still in its boot on the dead

28

horse and Edge had no way of reaching it without revealing his awareness. He had to assume that the sharp-shooter was good, not merely lucky and if that was so he would be able to loose off any number of accurate shots before Edge had even rolled over to look for the Henry. So Edge merely moved his right hand – on the blind side from the men – and discovered the only weapon within reach was a jagged, fist sized piece of rock. His fingers closed over it.

'Must of knocked himself out in the fall, Luke,' one of the men said excitedly.

'Damn rifle pulls to the right,' his partner replied with low anger. 'Way the Government is so close-handed, sometimes the horse is worth more than the outlaw.'

'He's facing this way, Luke,' the other said, refusing to have his enthusiasm quelled by Luke's chagrin. 'Recognise him? Wonder how much he's worth?'

Luke was tall and thin to the point of emaciation. He had hollow cheeks and deep-set eyes; a chin that came to a point. He was dressed all in black, from high-crowned hat to boots, and walked with a casual looseness. His partner was shorter, fat by comparison, with a round, moonlike face decorated with a moustache longer on one side than the other. He was all in black, too. Both carried rifles, wore revolvers in holsters on the right hip, tied at the thigh. Edge didn't recognise them as any of the many bounty hunters who worked out of Peaceville.

'Whoever it is, Chuck,' Luke said, raising his rifle, 'makes no difference whether he's dead or alive. Dead is easier for us.'

'Hey, no,' Chuck said with concern, reaching out a hand to slap down the rifle barrel. 'We don't even know if he's an outlaw. I told you not to shoot till he was close enough to take a look at.'

Luke sneered. 'Only two kind of lone riders in this part of the territory,' he said. 'Outlaws and bounty hunters. If he's one he's worth money, and it's easier money if he's dead. If he's the other he ain't no use to us living and dead he can't cause no trouble.'

Their voices got easier to hear as they got closer and Edge liked what they were saying less and less with every step they took.

'Hey,' Chuck exclaimed with glee when the pair were no more than five yards away, feet kicking up dust that threatened to erupt a sneeze from Edge. 'The guy's got one of them Henry repeating rifles. Confederates used to say the Union army could load on Sundays and keep firing all week with them.'

The man let his own, single shot weapon fall to the ground and rushed forward, sprang over the prone figure of Edge as if he presented no more danger than a solid rock. With Chuck out of his range of vision, Edge concentrated on Luke, who was the more dangerous of the two. He heard the Henry being slid from its boot, the breech mechanism worked.

'Terrific,' Chuck said, like a kid who got what he wanted for Christmas.

'Yeah,' Luke replied dully, but his eyes shone with an interest that belied his tone. Edge saw he carried an old and battered Spencer. He licked his lips as if he could taste the joy his partner was experiencing. He glanced down once at Edge, then stepped over him. 'Don't recognise him,' he said shortly. 'Let me see that gun.'

'It's mine,' Chuck said with petulance, then yelled in surprise.

Edge sprang into movement just as the tall man stepped over him. Forcing himself up from the ground with all the power in his arms to that his hard skull smashed into Luke's crotch. As Luke's cry of pain followed Chuck's yell, Edge continued the fast rise to his feet. The tall man grew taller, his legs straddling Edge's shoulder, then went crashing sideways as Edge turned, his outstretched hands clawing for Chuck to break his fall as his rifle dropped to the ground. But Chuck wasn't there. He went over backwards, stumbling against the dead horse as Edge released the jagged rock, sent it with a crunch of breaking bone into the little man's nose.

Luke hit solid earth with a great force that knocked the wind out of him, but he was tougher than he looked and he bounced to his feet, turning as he came up, facing Edge.

'Hundred dollars is all,' Edge said as Luke went for his Colt, never made it. Even without a backswing, Edge's leg shot forward with incredible speed and force, the toe of his boot finding

30

the exact spot where his head had landed moments before. Both Luke's hands streaked to his nether region as his knees buckled and his face took on a mask of pain. 'Figure I'm worth more,' Edge droned softly, hand snaking to his back, flashing out with the knife. Luke had sunk to his knees now, his mouth working to fight out words, failing. Edge held the knife low, pointing towards the injured man. Luke, eyes wide with horror, unable to tear his hands away from the source of his agony, rocked once and fell forward, his own weight carrying him on to the knife's needle point. It penetrated to great depth, just below his Adam's apple.

'Hey, don't get cut up about it,' Edge said as he withdrew the knife and pushed the dead body sideways, turned to find Chuck.

The little man was just getting to his feet, staring in pained surprise at the blood on his palm as he pulled his hand away from his mashed nose. His other hand was gripping the Henry by its barrel, which was the wrong place. He realised this when Edge spoke to him and he found himself looking into the muzzle of the Remington. They faced each other across the dead body of the horse.

'Chuck.'

'You was awake all the time?'

'Yeah, Chuck. That's my rifle you've got.'

'You killed Luke?'

'Luke killed my horse.'

Sweat mingled with blood. The moon face implored mercy. His voice trembled.

'You a bounty hunter?'

'No.'

'Outlaw?'

'Hundred dollars worth. My girl gave me that horse.'

He shot Chuck in the hand holding the Henry. The rifle clattered to the ground as Chuck screamed, his other hand going to nurse the injury. Edge shot that, too. Twice, blowing off two fingers and drilling a neat hole through the palm.

'Oh, God!' Chuck pleaded, and fell to his knees.

'Don't know how my girl felt about the horse, but I kind of liked it,' Edge said and emptied the revolver in a series of

CHAPTER SIX

SHE wasn't pretty. Examining her through his narrowed eyes, grinding his teeth in an expression of anger at allowing the woman to get the drop on him, Edge thought she was down-right ugly. She was tall, with a haggard, dirt-streaked face from which large, red-rimmed dark eyes looked at him with greedy interest. Her mouth was a mere thin line, pale pink against her sun-darkened skin and her long hair, the colour of dirty straw, hung limp and matted over her shoulders. Her dress was nothing more than a shapeless piece of grey rag that fell from the neck to ankles offering no hint at the form it covered. Only where it hugged the length of her long arms to be fastened at the wrists did it show her bone leanness. And the filthy hands below, curled around the gun she pointed at Edge, were just-skin-covered bones. She looked tired and weak, but her gun more than compensated for this at the distance she stood from Edge. It was one of the old Roland White Harmonica Rifles: a percussion repeater with a vertical sliding magazine. A sporting gun, but as effective against a man as an animal. And the woman held it like one not reluctant to use it. She stood beside a boulder behind which she had been concealed, lower down the slope from the point where Luke and Chuck had made their attack. Edge guessed she had moved down during the fight.

'Like what you see?' he asked.

Her deep-set eyes fastened upon his face for several moments, then began to travel down, halted with a flicker of surprise at his chest before continuing down to his feet. Then back to his chest.

'Why'd you say you had a hundred on your head?' she asked.

Edge glanced down, saw the star still pinned to his shirt

front. He grinned, jerked a thumb at the bodies of Luke and Chuck.

'Didn't want them to think they died trying for zero,' he answered. 'Friends of yours?'

'I rode with them,' she said shortly.

'Which one you sleep with?'

She wasn't insulted. 'They took turns.'

'I don't see you shedding tears.'

'Weeping women have no right in this part of the country,' she came back. 'Will anybody cry for you if I shoot you?'

Edge liked the word *if*. He thought fleetingly of Gail back in Peaceville, felt an odd kind of resentment that she would mourn him. She was a link with the past and he was a man for whom the past was a dead thing. It did not exist, so therefore must be dead – unless there were memories to keep it alive. The thought of Gail triggered off other recollections and Edge suddenly shut his mind to them. Now was what mattered: this woman with this gun discussing his death.

'Nobody,' he answered.

She nodded, happy with his answer. Perhaps feeling less alone because there was at least one other fellow human being on earth in similar circumstances. She raised the rifle and her finger whitened on the trigger as she drew a bead on the star. Edge prepared his muscles for a sideways leap, but suddenly the muzzle dropped and the rifle crack sent a bullet thudding into the ground between his spread feet.

'That's to show I could have plugged you good,' she told him, holding the rifle in one hand, low at her side, offering no threat.

Edge holstered the Remington and moved slowly across to her, grinning. Not until he stopped immediately in front of her, his head at the same height as her own, did she recognise the expression as a parody, saw the viciousness shining in the eyes. As one of his hands ripped the rifle from her grasp the other moved as a blur, back and forth, knuckles and palm slapping with force into each of her cheeks. She accepted the beating without flinching, her eyes dull, lips set in a firm line that barred any sound of pain. Finally, Edge stopped, breath-

34

ing deeply from the exertion, watching the bruises rise on her thin face.

'I met men like you before,' she said without emotion. 'They done worse than that to me.'

Edge nodded, acknowledging his belief of her words. A beating was not a new experience for this woman. Edge thought she had taken so many that she would miss them if they stopped.

'I get better as I go along,' Edge said wryly.

The woman shrugged her thin shoulders. 'I'm a woman and I got the better of you, a man. You couldn't let it rest. Where you headed, mister?'

The shot and the beating might never have happened. The words were spoken in a conversational tone, as if they were strangers who had met accidentally and were passing the time of day.

'My business,' Edge replied.

'I got no money and only a few supplies,' she answered. 'It's a bad country for a woman alone.'

Edge spat, and reached up his hand again, gently this time. His exploring fingers felt her scrawny neck, travelled down over her narrow shoulders, formed a cup over one small, hard breast, traversed the protrusions of her rib cage and halted on the taut flatness of her belly. She submitted tacitly to the assault of his hand. Like the beating, it was something she had been forced to accept many times before. Edge stepped back.

'I got delicate skin,' he said sardonically. 'I could cut myself on you.'

It got no reaction. 'I got other uses,' she said. 'I cook good and whenever you get mad at anything, you can beat me. You were going south when Luke made his play. I'm heading for Mexico.'

'I travel light.'

'I won't be no trouble.' For the first time the woman revealed a positive emotion, her features forming a tacit plea. 'Just to the next town.'

'What if there ain't no man there so hard-up he'd take you in?'

'I'll take my chances.'

35

'Go and get the horses,' Edge told her. 'Just the best two.'

She had been holding her breath for his decision, and let it out with a small gasp as she turned and started back up the slope, towards a craggy column of rock. Edge went over to the dead horse, unfastened her girth and dragged off his saddle and bedroll. He dusted off the Henry and was reloading the Remington when the woman emerged from around the rock, started down the slope leading two stallions, a big bay and a smaller piebald. They were both saddled, but carried no bed-rolls.

'What's your name?' Edge asked as the woman approached.

'Amy,' she answered.

'Pretty,' he said, holstering the Remington. 'Don't match your looks.'

'What's yours?'

'They call me Edge.'

'It suits,' she told him shortly.

Edge sat down, back against a rock and tipped his hat forward over his eyes, just enough so that he could see the lower half of her body, would know if she went for any of the dead men's guns or her own Harmonica which was resting across the back of the dead horse.

'Back up your claim to be a cook,' he told her. 'I don't like what you pull out of the pot, I'll slice off those hard little titties of yours and see if they tender in the cooking.'

He watched her ground tether the horses, then collect brush and make a fire. She got the makings of a meal from the saddlebags of the bay and water from the bottles on the pie-bald. Then she crouched down beside the pot and began to sing softly as she stirred its contents. Her speaking voice was harsh, with a rasp to it, but when she sang it took on a sweet-ness and clarity that caused Edge to raise his hat brim, look at her face. But he dropped it again, for she was still as ugly as ever.

> *As I walked out in the streets of Laredo,*
> *As I walked out in Laredo one day,*
> *I spied a poor cowboy all wrapped in white linen,*
> *All wrapped in white linen,*

> *As cold as the clay.*
> *I see by your outfit that . . .*

'You from Texas?' Edge asked, cutting off the woman in mid-song.

'No. Why?'

'That's where Laredo is.'

'I just like the song,' she answered, continuing to stir the pot, which was now giving off an appetising aroma that stirred Edge's taste buds. 'I'm from the state of Maine. How about you?'

'My business,' he answered and the woman bent over her cooking, choosing to hum rather than sing. Edge found himself almost hypnotised by the gentleness of the sound, felt his lids lowering and fought them up again several times before allowing the tune and the heat of the day to lull him into a shallow sleep.

He came out of it with the speed of a whip lash when fingers raised the brim of his hat, his hand streaking out to grip a thin wrist as his other hand flashed to the back of his neck, stayed there without drawing the razor when he heard the cry of half surprise, half pain, saw Amy's gaping mouth and wide eyes.

'Oh, lady . . .' he breathed.

'I got you unawares again,' she said. 'You want to hit me?'

He let go of her wrist, saw that in her other hand she held a metal bowl that steamed and gave off an aroma that raised saliva to his dry mouth.

'What is it?'

'Beef stew and potatoes,' she told him, thrusting the bowl forward. The spoon was already in it.

He took the food and began to eat as she straightened, hands on her hips. 'Well?' she asked, in a tone that indicated she already knew the verdict.

Edge grimaced. 'Not bad. Get away from me. Your ugly mug is spoiling my appetite.'

It was delicious.

The woman ate little, Edge scraping the pot clean. Then he mounted and set off, leaving her to rush the task of clearing the campsite, gallop in his wake before she lost sight of him.

When she did catch up with him, he on the bay, she astride the piebald, she rode alongside, keeping a distance of several feet between the two horses.

The heat did not seem to get any less as the afternoon lengthened, and the stew had been highly seasoned. Edge drank long and often from the canteens hung on the bay's saddle, emptied one and was halfway through the other before he noticed Amy's dry lips. He glanced at her canteens.

'Don't you get thirsty?'

'No,' she said, the words rattling in her parched throat.

Edge wheeled his horse and tugged on the reins, bringing him close to the woman. He reached out and under the dull, watchful eyes of Amy hooked her canteens clear, shook them one at a time and heard no sound from within. With a snort of rage he hurled them away and lashed out with his hand, his wrist chopping at the woman's throat. She gasped and fell backwards out of the saddle, feet coming clear of the stirrups so that she slid easily over the rump of the animal and thudded to the ground. He vaulted from his own mount and reached down for her, pulled her to her feet as her hands went to her throat and she gasped for breath.

'You stupid cow,' he hurled at her, and drove a fist into her stomach, doubling her over. 'Why didn't you tell me?'

'I . . . I . . . thought . . . ' she gasped, then went over sideways as Edge punched her on the side of the head.

'I been guzzling my water like there was a lake round every turn,' he yelled, launching a kick into the small of her back. 'I thought you had two full canteens.'

Amy looked up at him with the eyes of a faithful dog who knows the master's anger is well-deserved.

'I used my last for the stew,' she managed to force out through her pain. 'I didn't tell you. I thought you might leave me.'

'Lady, you thought right,' he told her and prepared to kick her again, held off when he saw she made no attempt to defend herself. He turned in disgust and walked to where his horse waited, climbed into the saddle. He shook his canteen, sighed when he heard the meagre sloshing of the short supply inside.

'I don't want no water,' Amy called, pulling herself to her

feet, still half doubled, one hand on her stomach, the other at her throat.

'You ain't getting any,' Edge spat at her, and heeled his mount forward into a fast gallop.

By the time the woman was able to haul her aching body up into the saddle of the piebald and encourage him forward, every step he took sending a fresh sweep of pain through her, Edge was just a dot in the distance, a black speck at the head of a long cloud of grey dust. She followed, noticing for the first time that Edge was following a trail, leaving single fresh tracks on top of the older sign of many horses.

Soon, the ground began to rise, become rockier, the old and new tracks more difficult to see. The figure in the distance was raising less dust and often went from sight as the terrain dipped and rose. With each mile Amy covered, her pain lessened, her ill-used body calling upon the experience of many past mistreatments to fight the effects of the latest onslaught. She was able to move faster and since the man ahead knew better than to push his mount at the limit for more than short stretches of country, she narrowed the distance that separated them. But she did not get too close. She endeavoured to maintain a gap just outside the rifle range and often she saw Edge turn in the saddle to look back at her but he made no move to come back or race ahead.

Once, she muttered, 'You bastard,' the words rasping out over her parched lips when she saw him raise the canteen to his mouth to drink in a gesture of torment.

But the afternoon was drawing to a close and the cool promise of evening offered her some relief. So she held her distance, afraid of facing a night alone in the desolate country, hating the man ahead but at the same time drawing comfort from his impassive back.

CHAPTER SEVEN

NIGHT pounced suddenly, like a thief to steal the light from the day, and toss it back as a pale luminescence which gave the terrain a freakish appearance, turning rock formations into frightening giants and the sparse vegetation into shapes of evil intent. Edge, a man with no imagination, found in the night only another difficulty: the tracks of the Mexican bandits already faint were even harder to see in the pale moonlight. But he kept moving, heading along a broad gully which he knew the men would have had to travel to continue their trek south.

It was cold now, the dry cold of the desert night which cuts through the thin clothes of those who travel with attire suitable only for the heat of the day. So Edge halted his horse near a cleft in the gully wall and untied his bedroll, took out a heavy blanket to drape around his shoulders. He had re-packed the roll when he heard the hoof beats coming up the gully, tossed it back across his mount when the woman's shout rang out. He grinned wryly, figuring the darkness scared her more than he did: that she was prepared to take anything he handed out just so long as she could be near him.

He waited, saw the white of the piebald's marking, then the paleness of the woman's face. The horse's shoes sent sparks flying as she reined him into a sliding, crabwise halt in front of Edge.

'We got company,' she said breathlessly, sliding from the saddle, showing no sign of her former pain.

Edge's eyes became hooded. 'How many?'

'Two.'

'Men?'

'Men.'

'How close?'

'Half a mile,' she answered sharply, then shrugged. 'Maybe less. Damn moonlight plays tricks with your eyes.'

'Riding fast?'

'Slow at first,' she breathed. 'Spotting our tracks. Then they saw me. Coming like bats out of hell now.'

Edge glanced around, saw the cleft. 'In here,' he commanded and led his own horse into the opening.

The woman came in close behind. Edge took the reins from her, unbooted the Henry and slid her rifle from his bedroll, tossed it to her. He beckoned for her to follow him and went out of the cleft, broke into a run to the opposite side of the gully, started to climb as the sound of thundering hoofs announced the approach of the newcomers. He reached a shelf of rock and stretched down a hand for the woman, hauled her up beside him.

'You're going to beat me again,' she said in a hushed whisper as the two riders appeared, galloped on down the gully then reined to a rearing halt as they realised the fresh tracks had disappeared. One of the horses in the cleft whinneyed and stamped a foot, the riders taking this as a signal to slide hurriedly from their saddles, unbooting their rifles with practised skill.

Edge watched them dive into shadow. 'Why so?' he asked in low tones.

'This gun,' she answered, laying it on the ground. 'The slug I put between your feet. It was the last one.'

Edge sighed. 'You're right.'

'What?'

'I'm going to beat you again.'

He had not moved his eyes off the patch of shadow where the men had taken refuge, saw movement now as one of them edged forward, going back towards the cleft where the horses now held their silence. He saw a glint of silver, high up. When the second man joined the first, a stray moonbeam produced the same effect.

'Somebody fingered me,' Edge muttered.

'What?' Amy asked.

'Those guys are marshals,' he answered absently. 'Wearing their tin on their hats.'

'You ain't the law then?'

'Not any more I ain't,' he told her, and ripped the badge from his shirt, pressed it into her hand. 'Here, have a souvenir.'

'Thanks a bunch.' She sneered. 'I'll treasure it and your memory 'til my dying day.'

'Maybe your day has come,' he said and squeezed the Henry's trigger.

The bullet spat chips from a rock close to the first marshal's face and he went into a crouch as his partner dived for the ground.

'Who's up there?' a voice called.

'Santa Claus come early this year,' Edge answered. 'Figure you won't be around come Christmas.'

'Funny,' Amy said drily.

'Shut up,' Edge told her.

'We're US territorial marshals,' the spokesman from below called. 'Your name Edge?'

'Close enough.'

'Throw down your gun and surrender,' came the response. 'We got a warrant for you. You'll get a fair trial. You'll have a better chance with us than with the bounty hunters.'

'You pass a couple of guys up north a ways?' Edge asked.

There was a pause. 'You?'

'I ain't admitting nothing, but they didn't die of pneumonia.'

'You kill me,' Amy said.

'How long you been telling fortunes?' he hissed from the side of his mouth.

Amy glanced at him, huddled beneath the blanket and refrained from further comment. His bitter humour was a mere surface veneer, a transparent cover for the brutal killer beneath.

'Give yourself up, Edge?' the marshal shouted.

Edge's answer was another rifle shot that drew a grunt of pain from below as it nicked skin from a creased brow. But the minor wound did not interfere with the man's aim as a hail of bullets whistled upwards, chipping rock from above and below the shelf, causing Edge to draw back, the woman

42

to roll herself into a ball. When the fusillade of firing died and Edge chanced a glance down he could no longer catch a glimpse of the lawmen. They had fired on the run, going for more secure places of concealment. A rifle cracked once and a flash from the cleft showed where it came from as Edge ducked back.

He decided they had split up and that he would not see or hear from one of them until he was in a position to make a kill. Edge looked to his left and right, saw that the shelf upon which he and the woman were crouched narrowed away to nothing in one direction, continued flat and broad in the other. He looked up and saw a sheer face. Over to his right the incline got less steep, became potted with indentations, was host to some thick clumps of brush. Below, the marshal in the cleft opened up again and a hail of bullets forced Edge to interrupt his surveillance, draw back to the rear of the protective shelf. When the marshal had emptied his gun, took time to reload, Edge glanced to his right again, saw the second lawman running at a crouch up the slope, duck behind some brush.

'I ain't been smart,' he muttered.

'We trapped?' the woman asked.

'They know their jobs,' he admitted grudgingly.

'I ain't wanted by the law,' she said.

'I'm fresh out of sympathy,' Edge told her and pressed the Remington into her hand, not taking his eyes off the brush where the marshal was hiding. 'When I give the signal, pour lead down on to that guy below. Don't stop until the gun's empty.'

'I don't want to shoot no lawman,' she told Edge.

'They die as easy as anybody else,' he said, and dug his elbow into her skinny side. 'Now.'

She opened up without aiming, just pushing the gun over the edge of the shelf and firing. Up on the right the second marshal mistook the first few shots for covering fire and came clear of the brush, took three fast paces out into the open towards a cluster of rocks before he saw the flashes coming from the wrong place.

He didn't live to learn by his error. He fired on the turn, his bullet whining low along the shelf, ricocheting, tugging at Edge's blanket, spraying rock chippings into his face. Edge fired three times before the marshal had completed his turn-about. The first bullet ploughed a deep furrow across his chest, the second took him in the ear and the third went into his back, lodged in his lungs and sent him sprawling in death towards the brush he had so desired in life.

Silence was a heavy weight settling on the gully, pressing against the ears and intensifying the coldness.

'Ned?' the marshal below shouted, the name coated with concern. 'You okay, Ned?'

'I'm dead,' Edge whispered, pressing his lips against the woman's ear. 'You tell him that. You say you're innocent and tell him to hold his fire.'

'I don't know if . . .'

Edge dug his teeth into the lobe of her ear and she squealed in pain. 'Lady, you do what I tell you, and then you do what he tells you.'

'Ned?'

'Edge killed him,' the woman called, a tremor in her voice so that it barely sounded above a whisper.

'What?'

'The other man's dead,' she answered, louder now. 'They killed each other.'

'A woman?' the marshall said in surprise. 'That a woman up there?'

'It's the way I was born,' she answered. 'Did you hear what I said? They're both dead.'

'I don't believe you.' A pause. 'Not about Edge.'

'Throw down the revolver,' Edge hissed.

'Look, here's his gun,' she called, and her arm arced. The Remington clattered down the side of the gully, bounced and thudded to the bottom.

'He had a rifle,' the marshal shouted.

Edge picked up the empty Harmonica and thrust it into her hands.

'Here it comes.'

The rifle went the way of the Remington, making more noise. Moments of silence, then:

'Who are you?'

'Name's Amy Ridgeway. Edge picked me up on the desert. I had supplies and I cooked for him. I didn't know he was no outlaw, mister. I'd have known that, I wouldn't have rode with him.'

'Show yourself.'

She shot a scared glance at Edge, small pointed teeth gnawing at her lower lip. 'I'm scared,' she whispered. 'He might shoot at me.'

'Take your pick,' Edge told her. 'The lawman might. I will.'

She drew in her breath, knew he was not making an idle threat. 'I'm going to stand up, mister,' she called. 'I ain't armed.'

'Make it slow and easy,' the lawman instructed.

The woman pressed herself against the rock face at the back of the shelf and inched her way up, holding her breath. When she was standing erect, seemingly frozen against the rock face with her face a mask of fear in the pale moonlight, Edge inched forwards.

'Move so he can see you,' he whispered.

'I can't,' she hissed back at him. 'I can't move a muscle.'

'I'll help you,' he said, swung up the Henry and jabbed the muzzle hard between her legs, felt it sink in.

The woman gave a low moan. Edge grinned wryly. 'You just been screwed by Henry,' he said.

'You kill me,' she muttered, stepping forward.

'Yeah,' he said, rolled on to his side and kicked out. His boots hooked around her calves and she stumbled forward, a scream of alarm leaping from her throat as she went off the shelf, smashed her skull on a projection of rock and cartwheeled down to the floor of the gully, the snapping of bones accompanying the dull thud of her body as it completed each turn.

'Have a good trip, Amy,' Edge murmured when the final thud announced her fall had ended.

The silence then was solid enough to cut with a knife. The cold bit deeper and Edge wrapped the blanket around his body more securely, prepared to wait for as long as the marshal deemed safe.

'Edge?'

It wasn't what Edge wanted to hear.

'Edge, you up there?'

Edge grinned into the darkness. He kept his breathing low and did not move a muscle. There was a vocal sound from below: one word that was inaudible in meaning but said in a tone that meant the marshal had cursed. Silence for long moments, then a slap of hand on horse flesh, a whinney and pounding of hoofs. One of the animals, either the bay or the piebald, galloped away down the gully. Edge didn't look to see which one. It wasn't the right sound. Then, after another long pause, came the unmistakable crunch of a human footfall on hard rock. Pause. Another footfall. The marshal was making slow progress out of the cover of the cleft of the rocks. Edge raised his eyebrows in surprise, figured the lawman had taken no more than fifteen minutes to make his move. But Edge remained absolutely immobile, knowing that nervous eyes would be focussed upon the shelf, an anxious finger curled around a trigger.

Then the footsteps sounded closer together as the man moved more quickly. Then they stopped and Edge counted to three and shot himself forward on his elbows, angling the Henry down the steep slope. The marshal heard the sounds and came up from his stoop over the woman, face clouding with horror.

'Drop it,' Edge commanded and the man complied, his rifle thudding to the ground.

'You pushed her?'

'She didn't have a lot to live for. Who put you on to me?'

'Liveryman recognised your picture on the wanted poster,' the marshal answered. 'Waitress at the restaurant said you'd headed north. Her boss backed her up. We figured they were lying.'

'Obliged,' Edge said and shot him, cleanly through the heart. The man collapsed on to the woman in an embrace of death.

Edge rose, draped the blanket around himself and started down the slope. He didn't even glance at the bodies as he crossed to the cleft, discovered it had been the bay the marshal had spooked to try to flush him out. He found his Remington and walked slowly down to where the lawmen's two horses waited patiently. He selected the big chestnut mare with a new saddle. Each horse carried a canteen, both half full and he tipped one into the other. Then he reloaded both the Remington and the Henry and mounted, urged the animal forward, south again.

> *Oh beat the drum slowly, and play the fife lowly*
> *Play the dead march as you carry me along.*

He tried to finish the song which Amy had sung, but could not recall the final lines, so hummed it to its conclusion.

'Five more including two lawmen,' he said pensively to his unattentive horse. 'Guess I must be piling quite a bounty on my head. Be glad when I cross the border.'

CHAPTER EIGHT

HALF a night's ride ahead of Edge, El Matador and his bandits approached the Mexican village of San Murias in the cold early hours. It was the way of their brutal leader to attack his objectives at such a time. For, he reasoned, that at such an hour a raid was never expected, and those who might attempt retaliation were at their most unready. Sleep robbed a man of his defences and in the few seconds it took him to realise his danger, a bullet or a blade could despatch him with a simplicity that placed every advantage with the attacker.

Matador and eighteen of his men went into the village on foot, leaving two to attend the horses. There were not more than a dozen buildings in the settlement, most of them rude shacks providing squalid living quarters for the poor peasants who sweated to earn a living from the arid soil to the west. One, a little larger, was a cantina and another, larger still, a storage barn for farm produce. The reason the settlement had been built in that particular place was a well that had been bored down in the very centre of the square around which the buildings rose.

Not a light showed as the bandits crept into the square, forming a group around the well. And they made not a sound, their leader indicating with a stab of his finger his plan of campaign. As their turn came, each bandit broke from the group and moved swiftly over to a house until each door was flanked by dark, evil looking figures, rifles at the ready. Finally, Matador was alone in the square's centre and as he stooped to haul up the bucket from the well the bandits leapt in front of the doors and kicked them open, firing at random into the inky blackness beyond.

Cries of alarm and screams of agony echoed the cracks of rifle shots as the bandits crashed into the houses. While, in the centre of the square as if in the heat of a peaceful summer's day, Matador pulled the bucket clear of the well and pressed his face into it, sucking up the icy, clean tasting water. As he drank, his eyes watched over the rim of the bucket and he saw a naked man run from an open doorway, a shot from inside whining over the head of the retreating figure. Without interrupting his drinking, Matador swivelled his right holster and squeezed the trigger of the Colt. The man flung forward his hands and went to the ground, lay unmoving. Matador, his thirst assuaged, dropped the bucket and heard it splash into water far below. Then he spun slowly on his heels, eyes going from one doorway to the next around the square as the surviving occupants of the houses were herded outside. There were men, women and children showing varying degrees of terror. More women than men, most of them young for not all the shots had been wild ones. A few children because some of the bandits retained a steak of sentimentality.

When he had turned full circle, Matador went halfway round again, his eyes fastening upon a tall girl of some sixteen years with long black hair and a beautiful face marred by a red welt on her cheek. He strode arrogantly across to her, found his face came on a level with the breasts which thrust forward under the rough thickness of her long nightgown. She looked down at him with fear-filled eyes. He stepped back a pace, hooked the muzzle of his blunderbuss under the hem of the gown and raised it as high as her stomach. The girl's legs trembled as the bandit leader examined her body with lustful interest.

'Your name, girl?' he demanded, letting the gown fall back, feasting his eyes upon the still-concealed breasts.

'Maria,' she said hoarsely.

'Pretty, like you. Except for the mark. Who hit you?'

The girl glanced to her left, where her father stood, frustrated anger twisting his handsome face.

'I did,' he blurted out, taking a step forward. 'For showing her body to another pig of a man last night.'

Matador raised the blunderbuss, halting the man.

'Who?'

'Filipe Manola.'

'He is dead,' a woman cried from across the square. 'My son. My son Filipe is dead. You have killed him.'

Matador made a face. 'It is a pity. I like to kill my rivals myself. Maria is mine.'

As the charge from the blunderbuss cut the girl's father in half, Maria's body was suddenly naked with the downward rip of Matador's fingers. She screamed and it was the signal for an orgy of killing and rape as men and children and old women were blasted into death before the bandits pounced upon the girls, ripping the nightwear from their bodies and driving them to the ground.

Some of the girls screamed and fought vainly against the hysterical lust of the men while others submitted frigidly to the attack. Hands smashed into faces to demand an end to resistance and those bandits who had to wait their turn yelled encouragement at the others who sweated upon their victims, thrusting their lust into unwilling bodies.

One man, incensed by the constant screaming of a twelve-year-old girl drew his revolver and fired it into her open mouth.

From one of the houses emerged a man, his left arm shot away at the shoulder, dragging up a heavy rifle with his good hand. His horror-filled eyes roved the square, fastened upon the spread-legged figure of his daughter as a second raper was about to straddle her. He knew he would only be able to get off one shot and he took aim, praying to heaven for an accurate bullet. It was answered. The shot hit the girl in the side of the head, releasing her from further agony a moment before her father went down in a hail of revolver fire from the furious bandits.

Their sexual lust spent, the bandits were engulfed by another kind of desire. Matador again provided the signal, rising from Maria and whipping out his Colts in a two handed draw, crossing his forearms and drilling a hole down through each of her firm, young breasts. Torres slashed open the throat of his girl just as he reached climax and Miguel sliced off both breasts of another girl with a forward and backward flash of a sabre. Other bandits contented themselves with emptying their rifles and revolvers into naked flesh.

The stillness after the carnage was suddenly filled with the heavy, exhausted breathing of the satiated bandits as they surveyed the scene before them. But Matador allowed them only seconds in which to recover.

'Food and tequila,' he shouted. 'Then we ride for Hoyos.'

The square burst into movement again as the bandits went on the run back into the hovels that comprised the greater part of the village. There was no shooting this time because the men found nothing at which to shoot. Instead, the houses exploded with the sound of hurried, careless search as the marauders sought supplies. And soon, as Matador watched from his position in the square's centre, they emerged with the little they had found. Only the four who had chosen to raid the tiny cantina had difficulty in carrying what they had – many bottles of tequila and dark red wine.

From the hayloft in the barn, Luis Aviles looked down upon the looters and their dead victims, his eyes shining with excitement and his lips parted in a smile of relish. The loft was Luis' home and had been for many years, ever since he had first come to San Murias. It smelled of hay and horse-dung and of Luis himself, for as he grew older he became less fastidious about his personal cleanliness and Luis was very old. As near as he could calculate, he was seventy. He was small and slightly built, with a wizened face burned almost black by the sun. It was a dull face, with small, matt black eyes and an unexpressive mouth, framed by surprisingly thick bláck hair, fringed over the forehead. A face that surveyed his world of the hayloft and the cantina – where he earned a pittance of pesos for sweeping the floor – with a constant expression of sourness. Only when his feeble brain recalled the events of the past did his face become animated and he needed a strong cue to set his recollections into motion. The scene below him, as he peered through a knot hole in the front of the barn, was an ideal memory aid for it was a repetition of many such raids in which he had been involved.

He had seen the whole thing, from the stealthy arrival of Matador and his bandits – the forced entry into the houses, the shooting of those villagers who had no sexual attraction for the attackers, the rapes and murder of the girls and now the

51

looting. He had watched every moment and every move, his mind participating via his greedy eyes in the events he knew his body would never again enjoy. His admiration for Matador knew no bounds. For Lius Aviles had ridden with many bandit groups, but never had he seen before an attack carried out with such skill and disregard for human life.

As the horses were brought up and the food and drink packed away there was just one thing which nagged at Luis' mind. The bandits had done something wrong, or perhaps had neglected something. Luis' face took on even more creases as he puzzled over the irksome doubt, but as the men in the square swung astride their mounts and prepared to ride out, Luis had to shake his head in perplexity.

Matador, mounted at the head of the column of bandits, suddenly took off his sombrero with a sweeping gesture and bowed in the saddle to three sides of the square, across the untidy litter of dead bodies.

'El Matador thanks the people of San Murias for their hospitality,' he said in sardonic tones.

'Especially the ladies,' Miguel put in and the night was suddenly noisy with laughter, to be drowned by the thud of hoofbeats as the horses were heeled into a canter.

Dust rose in clouds as the riders went south, and Luis remained in concealment until the sound had died into the distance and the dust had settled. Then he pulled himself to his feet, his movements slow with age, and went down through a hole in the loft floor, using a ladder to descend to ground level. He opened the barn door just a crack to peer outside. Nothing moved and after he had waited for a full minute, he went out. Excitement shone in his features again as he moved among the bodies. He smiled with satisfaction as he looked into the dead face of the cantina owner who had paid him so cheaply; he kicked the head of the ugly woman who charged him a week's wages to come into the loft and spread her flaccid body beneath his; he showed a parody of regret as he stooped over the headless body of a young girl and cupped his bony fingers over a breast that was already cold and beginning to set into rigor.

Not until he had finished his exploration, went to sit with

his back against the cantina wall and lift to his lips a bottle of tequila that the bandits had dropped, did his mind lock on to the reason for the stab of anxiety he had experienced as the raiders took their leave. He, Luis Aviles, was the only citizen of San Murias left alive. For several moments his body trembled at the realisation. But then he spat and his mouth took on a grin.

'El Matador,' he shouted aloud. 'I no longer admire you. In the old days we would have made sure nobody was left to tell the tale.'

Then he raised the bottle and drank long and deep, enjoying the warmth of the liquid as it combated the cold of the night. It had been many years since he had been able to drink a whole bottle and now, as he took advantage of his good fortune, the fire inside him burned bright, was not extinguished until it consumed his mind and he toppled sideways into drunken oblivion.

CHAPTER NINE

WHEN Edge rode into San Murias just as the sun of the new day was beginning to reach the full promise of its heat, Luis Aviles was no longer against the cantina wall. Thus, the hooded eyes of the lone rider saw only death in its many forms spread across the square. He looked at the scene impassively, giving his horse free rein to pick her way among the scattered bodies, offered no command until he reached the well, when he called a halt and slid to the ground. The big mare stood obediently as Edge spun slowly on his heels, his eyes fastening momentarily upon each open doorway, moved on when nothing could be seen beyond. Only when he was satisfied that San Murias was a village of the dead, did Edge step up to the well and begin to haul on the rope to bring the water filled bucket to the top. Just as El Matador had drunk only hours before, Edge pushed his face into the bucket and sucked up the cool, refreshing liquid.

'You move, Americano, and you're as dead as everybody else in this accursed place.'

Edge froze at the sound of the voice, speaking in slow Spanish, coming from over on his right. But he continued to drink, swivelling his eyes and tipping the bucket slightly. Reflected in its surface he saw the blurred shape of Luis standing in the barn doorway, aiming a rifle.

'I've drunk my fill,' he called.

'Your horse looks thirsty, señor.'

Edge straightened, then stooped to place the bucket on the dusty ground. The chestnut mare pushed her snout into it. Edge looked across at the old man, saw him as a slight figure in tattered pants and scuffed boots, the top half of his body draped in a much torn poncho.

'You kill them?' he asked.

Luis shook his head sadly. 'Many times have I wanted to, but a man needs much speed to do such a thing. I am an old man and slow.' He sniggered. 'But fast enough to shoot one man.'

'Why kill me?' Edge asked.

'That is a fine animal you have, señor,' Luis replied. 'There is nothing more for me in San Murias and I must travel. A horse, she is much better than a burro. There are only burros here.'

There was no shade in the centre of the square and Edge was beginning to tire of the direct heat of the sun and of the old man. He sighed.

'If you just put the rifle down, old man,' he said, 'I may not kill you. If you do not drop it I am going to count to three and then I will kill you. I'm not old, and I am very fast.'

His tone was low and easy, his voice just carrying to the barn where the old man strained his failing hearing to make sense of the words. Age, the effects of the tequila, and a fear of Edge caused his hands to shake, so that the rifle muzzle wavered.

'You talk tough, Americano,' he said, and the shake was audible in his voice.

'One,' Edge called and drew in a blur, squeezing the trigger of the Remington.

With a yell of alarm Luis threw the rifle into the air and in the instant the revolver's firing mechanism slid into movement Edge altered his aim. The bullet smashed into the rifle's stock, kicking the big gun into a spin before it thudded to the ground.

'You said three,' Luis called, affronted.

'Sometimes I tell lies,' Edge answered, holstering the revolver, kicking the bucket into the well as his horse finished drinking.

'Americanos have no honour.'

Edge grinned coldly, lifted the chestnut's reins and led her towards the shade of the barn. 'Honour is for the young who want to die that way. I figure to live a long time.'

He grimaced when he smelled the man, moved to one side

of him and glanced out of the shadow into the body littered square.

'El Matador?'

Luis nodded. 'That is what his men called him. Very small.' He held up a hand, indicating the height of the bandit chief. 'But a big leader. Many men. They come quietly, like mountain lions stalking prey. Then, boom, boom. The people do not know what is happening until they are dead.' He grinned. 'Except for the girls. The bandits, they let the girls live for a little longer. For just long enough, you know?' He winked and leered knowingly.

Edge eyed him coldly and the look withered the old man's enjoyment of the memory. 'You're all that's left?'

Luis spat. 'Like you, señor, I wish to live many more years. I hide and I watch. I know the ways of bandits. Once I was a bandit. We were the most feared in all Mexico. Fast, like you, I was. I have killed many men. Had many women. More than El Matador will enjoy, for he is careless. After a thing like San Murias, nobody should be left alive to tell the tale.'

Edge did not appear to be listening. He had drawn his knife and was idly paring his nails. Then his eyes found Luis' face. 'What's your name?'

'Luis Aviles, señor,' came the reply. 'I rode with . . .'

'You saw it all?'

'Everything, señor.'

'And heard?'

His eyes shone. 'The shooting. And the screams of the girls.'

'Must have been fun,' Edge said drily. 'Did you hear any words?'

'Words, señor?'

'Did they say where they were headed when they left here?'

An enthusiastic nodding of his head. 'They ride for Hoyos, señor. I heard El Matador say this. For Hoyos. Señor, you wish to follow the bandits?'

'I ain't in Mexico for my health,' Edge replied, speaking more to himself than to the old man. 'Where is Hoyos?'

Luis pointed a crooked finger towards the south. 'Many miles, señor. In the mountains, high up. An evil place where many bandits have lived. I lived there once. Sometimes the

56

soldiers come and there is much fighting. But always the bandits return. A man has to be a brave one to go to Hoyos alone.'

'I ain't going alone, Luis,' Edge said and turned on an icy grin when he saw the look of bewilderment on the other's face.

'Señor?'

'Following tracks is tiring work, Luis,' Edge explained. 'You know where Hoyos is, so you can take me.'

Luis shook his head emphatically. 'I do not want to go, señor. It is a bad place. El Matador is a bad man.'

Edge finished working on his nails and held the knife out in front of him, turning it so that the blade flashed sunlight. Luis squinted his eyes against the dazzle.

'My Spanish ain't so good, I guess,' Edge said. 'You don't understand, Luis. I wasn't asking you to come along . . . I was telling you, amigo.'

'Please . . . ?' Luis implored.

Edge looked about the square. 'There's nothing here for you. I couldn't leave you here like this. In a village of the dead there is no place for a man who lives. I'd feel obliged to kill you, Luis. You coming?'

'I think I come with you, señor,' Luis answered, and now his nod was as emphatic as the head shaking had been. 'I will lead you to Hoyos and then you will be grateful and release me to go my own way.'

'Where would you go, Luis?'

'To a place I know where there is much money, señor,' came the reply, and again a memory animated the crinkled face. 'Money that is all mine.' Then something triggered a stronger recollection and he stared with glowing eyes at a crudely designed ring on the third finger of his right hand. 'Ten thousand, American,' he said in a hushed tone of reverence.

Edge swung himself into the saddle and looked down at the old man without emotion. 'Get your burro, old man,' he said. 'When we get to Hoyos I will decide whether to let you go in search of your dream.'

Luis looked up at the tall, lean American, resenting the remark. 'It is not a dream, señor,' he replied. 'The money is

57

mine and when I get it, I will be almost as rich as El Presidente himself.'

'Get the burro,' Edge snapped at him. 'Or I ride to Hoyos
alone.'

The old man suddenly grinned his approval of this arrange-
ment, but the cold look on Edge's face thrust into his dull brain
the knowledge of what would happen to him if the tall man
left San Murias alone. He scuttled around the side of the
barn, with Edge behind him, to where a half-dozen mangy
burros were tethered. He cut out the best of a bad bunch and
mounted, bare-backed.

Edge nodded towards the south. 'You lead, Luis. You know
the way and also I will be upwind of you.'

'Señor?' Luis was bewildered.

'Move,' Edge barked. 'Find a friend to tell you.'

CHAPTER TEN

AFTER many attempts to start a conversation with the taciturn Edge, the Mexican peasant lapsed into a disgruntled silence, except when he had to drive his mount forward on the many occasions when the animal became reluctant to continue the journey. For his part, Edge was content to jog along at what was a snail's pace compared to the hard riding he had been doing to this point. He knew his destination and he believed what Luis had told him about Hoyos as a refuge for El Matador and his men. It seemed to grow hotter with every mile they travelled south and the slow pace set by the irrascible burro was therefore to be welcomed in terms of conserving strength and energy for whatever lay ahead.

They provided an odd sight as they traversed the parched, sun-bleached terrain of northern Mexico. The old man hunched over the small burro, chin resting on his chest, head hidden beneath the wide-brimmed sombrero, body lost under the drape of the poncho, legs hanging low on each side so that his feet often hit the ground where it humped. Behind him, high and erect on the back of the big chestnut horse, the tall, lean American riding with a blank expression of his bearded face, just the top half in shadow from his hat brim. In this shadow gleamed the two slits which were his eyes, watchful out of narrowed lids, reconnoitring the country ahead.

Luis had spoken the truth when he said that Hoyos was many miles to the south, for they had to ride throughout the entire day and it was long after nightfall when the old man pulled in his rope reins and slid to the ground, looked back at Edge.

'You tired?' Edge demanded, his tone warning that an affirmative answer would signal a violent reaction.

'Señor,' Luis said. 'Hoyos is up there.'

He pointed, and Edge looked in the direction indicated. They were in high country now, had been climbing steadily since before the sun slid behind the western horizon. They were in the Sierra Madre range which reached down the western side of Mexico and through the length of Central America to link the Rockies in the north to the Andes in the south. Often, Luis had hesitated as they climbed, apparently undecided upon the direction to take when more than one route was revealed. But the skills learned in his violent younger days stood him in good stead and when he finally called the halt there was confidence, tinged with pride, in the fact that he had led the American where he wanted to go.

Looking up, Edge could see a narrow trail winding across the face of what at first appeared to be a sheer cliff of rock, towards a plateau at the top. But the rock face had a slight incline sufficient for the trail to zig-zag to the top, only wide enough to allow passage for one rider.

'You see why the bandits like it, señor,' Luis said. 'The mountains beyond are impassable. This is the only way into the town. The soldiers are able to attack only when the fools above are too drunk to watch for attack. My good wishes, señor. El Matador will surely kill you, but it is customary to wish an amigo luck, even when he attempts the impossible.'

Luis urged his burro to the side of the trail and gave Edge an exaggerated bow to usher him by.

'Luis,' Edge said softly, without moving forward.

Luis looked up, the tone in which his name had been spoken raising fear to his face. 'Señor?'

'It is customary for me to kill men who do not do what I ask,' Edge said.

'But my money? My ten thousand, American.' His voice was plaintive.

'Your life is not worth more?' Edge asked easily.

The old man seemed on the verge of arguing the point, but then he sighed. 'Truly, you have no honour, señor.'

Edge grinned. 'Truly I have not,' he agreed and heeled his horse forward after Luis had mounted and started up the narrow trail.

The going got steeper as they rose higher, the unprotected

edge of the trail presenting a terrifying prospect of an un-hampered drop to a crushing death should burro or horse put a foot wrong.

'Señor?' Luis called from ahead.

Edge grunted a response.

'What if El Matador has a guard posted?'

'You are in front,' Edge told him laconically. 'The guard will kill you first.'

He heard the old man swallow hard, and there was no fur-ther talk from him. At the top the trail broadened a little, just before it reached up for the final stretch to the lip of the plateau. Edge dismounted and unbooted the Henry. Luis remained seated on the burro, trying to control the trembling which shook his body as he watched the American creep for-ward, peer around a clump of brush that grew thick and thorny at the top of the trail. Once he glanced over his shoulder, contemplated making a run for it. But he knew he would be either shot or fall off the edge before he could make more than a few yards on the slow beast between his legs. He spat.

Edge looked at Hoyos, his face showing no sign of how he felt about the prospect before him. It stood back from the lip of the plateau, some five hundred yards, concealed from below. And, as Luis had said, the mountains towered behind it, making it impossible to approach from the south. The terrain to the east and west was hidden in darkness, but Edge thought it possible that sheer rock faces fell away to form other natural defences for the town. But the pioneer citizens of Hoyos had not been content to leave their protection from attack entirely to the good fortune of nature. All Edge could see of the town was a twenty-feet-high wall of adobe, gleaming white in the pale moonlight, with a yawning gap of darkness which was an open gateway. Through and beyond he could see nothing, and there was a silence hulking over the walled town, almost tangible in its completeness.

Edge drew back and turned to Luis. 'Get off,' he demanded.

The old Mexican did as he was bid and when Edge snapped his fingers, led the burro forward. The tall man took the rope reins and urged the beast to the top of the trail. Then he walked behind the animal and jabbed the rifle muzzle hard into its rump. The burro snorted with injured rage, kicked out viciously with its hind legs and bolted across the open ground towards Hoyos. Crouching behind the brush, Edge peered towards the gateway and then flicked his eyes along the flat top of the walls on either side. The only sign and sound of life in the whole vista was the angry burro, which bolted through the gateway and was suddenly lost from sight. Soon, too, the sound of its hoofs disappeared.

'There is nobody in Hoyos,' Luis said in a hoarse whisper as he squatted beside Edge.

'You wanna bet?' Edge asked without breaking his concentrated examination of the town.

'Señor?'

'Maybe they all got tired and went to sleep,' Edge said absently.

'No, señor,' Luis said in all seriousness. 'Hoyos never sleeps. It has cantinas with much tequila, many girls. When the bandits ride in there is a fiesta. Much noise . . . Drinking, women, some fights. Knives and guns. Sometimes there is killing. If some sleep, there are always others who are awake.'

'How long since you been here?' Edge asked.

'Many years,' Luis said with a shrug.

'Maybe the reformers have moved in.'

'Maybe,' Luis allowed without conviction.

'Let's try again,' Edge muttered. 'On your feet, amigo.'

'Señor?'

'Nobody's going to waste a bullet on a burro. A man, that's different.'

'You would not make me do it,' Luis said, beginning to tremble again.

Edge sighed. 'Put it this way, amigo. You take a slow walk over to the gate and there's a chance you won't be killed. Keep squatting here and there ain't any doubt of it.'

There was a rustle of movement and Edge was holding the knife, its point pressed against the old man's grizzled throat.

'I do not like you, señor,' Luis said.

'When I run for mayor, I won't count on your vote,' Edge told him. 'Move it, amigo.'

Luis, every muscle in his body trembling as from a great

cold, got shakily to his feet, hesitated and then stepped from the cover of the brush, began to drag his feet towards the gate. Edge watched him for a few moments, then flicked his attention to the town.

'I am unarmed!' the old man suddenly shouted, and thrust his arms out on each side of him. 'See. My burro he bolted from me and now I come to claim him. Do not shoot an unarmed man, amigos.'

Edge's lips tightened in a snarl. If the people of Hoyos were asleep the progress of a runaway burro would cause them no alarm. But the whining pleas of the old man were a different matter. However, the impassive walls of Hoyos with the chasm of blackness at their centre offered no response to the shouting, beyond acting as a sounding board to throw back the frightened wails.

'Hold it there, amigo,' Edge called suddenly when the old man was within twenty yards of the gateway.

Luis halted abruptly, body still trembling, teeth chattering against each other as he strained his eyes to peer into the darkness above. Behind him he heard Edge cluck to his horse, then the sounds of footfalls and hoof treads as man and animal approached him.

'Maybe El Matador got randy again,' Edge whispered to Luis. 'Reckon you been asking the dead not to kill you?'

'I can feel a thousand eyes watching me, señor,' the old man said throatily.

'They all belong to your guilty conscience,' Edge told him and jabbed him in the back with the rifle muzzle.

The two men went forward, reached the dark opening and entered. After the moonlight which had bathed the plateau outside the walls, it was like entering a dark cave on a sunlit day. Luis heard Edge halt behind him, to take time to adjust his eyes, and he did likewise.

'Señor?'

Edge grunted.

'I cannot see any bodies.'

'Don't feel bad about it,' came the reply, punctuated by the crack of a rifle shot. The bullet kicked dust a few inches in front of Luis' boots, but he yelled as if it had pierced his flesh. Edge tightened his grip on the Henry as his eyes flicked over the dark shapes of buildings. He had seen the flash of the shot, knew the exact point from where it had been fired. But the sharpshooter was obviously not alone. Equally obviously, he could have shot to kill had he wanted to.

'There are just the two of you?' a voice said from another direction, cutting across the snivelling of the old man.

'How many you expecting?' Edge called back.

'We have a bullet for every bandit in the area,' the disembodied voice answered flatly, and then became part of a whole as a match flared and a face leapt out of the darkness.

It was a young, handsome face with dark eyes and full lips, finely chiseled chin and high cheekbones. In the flame as it touched the end of a long, thin cigar, it was a face topped by a cap with a shiny peak. Below, on the edge of the area of flickering light, could be seen the uniformed collar and shoulders bearing the insignia of a captain in the Mexican Federal army. It was a face with an insolent smile that almost invited Edge to loose off a shot at it. But then other lights flared, and were touched to torches, blazing into life all around the wide plaza that was spread just inside the town gate. Each torch was held high by a Mexican soldier and each of these soldiers was joined by another who aimed a rifle. Edge allowed his Henry to clatter to the ground as his eyes completed a hundred and eighty degree turn and estimated a detachment of about fifty men.

'Señor,' said Luis with a tremor. 'I think we are caught like the mice in the trap.'

'Yeah,' Edge answered. 'And the cat that's got us looks real hungry.'

CHAPTER ELEVEN

THE cell stank of the fear of every man who had been thrown into it. This smell was released from every piece of straw that was moved beneath the feet, burst out of the rancid blankets on the wooden bunk like some evil perfume and seemed to ooze out of the thick adobe walls like condensation on a cold day. It appeared to be intensified by the darkness of the tiny room and as Edge rose from where he had been thrown by the two soldiers who had marched him from the plaza, he drew consolation from the fact that the stench covered the vile odour which emanated from Luis Aviles. The Mexican lay in the far corner, stunned or perhaps too petrified to move after he had been flung bodily into the cell. The stout wooden door slammed shut and four pairs of booted feet marched away down the corridor outside. Some sharp commands were rattled off, sounding far in the distance, and then silence descended once more on Hoyos.

Edge sat on the bunk and breathed deeply for several long moments, regaining the wind which had been knocked out of him. It had been quick and efficient, the officer not having to utter a word as four soldiers had moved forward from the ring of light. Two had disarmed Edge of his revolver and knife while the others searched Luis without result. Then the march across the plaza, speed encouraged by rifle muzzles jabbed painfully into the kidneys. An open doorway in a large, solid structure that might once have been a church. Along a corridor. Luis picked up and hurled into the cell, the larger Edge sent stumbling inside with a boot in the small of his back.

'Señor?' A rustling of straw, a groan as a bruised muscle was brought into action.

Edge grunted.

'It is so quiet.'

'Let's keep it that way.'

But Luis had counted as many soldiers as Edge, and his fear of the tall American was diminished in relation to the menace of the uniformed men. Edge's steel-plated words were no longer sufficient to terrorise the old man into silence.

'What are they waiting for?'

Edge sighed, knowing the only way to discourage Luis was to ignore him. He thought he knew why the Captain was maintaining silence. He did not trust the fact of two men alone. The detachment had obviously been deployed in expectation of the arrival of many men. The way Edge had chosen to announce his arrival at the town indicated, perhaps, that he was a scout for a large group. Such a group, by the nature of the trail up the slope, would have to be waiting below, would not have seen the light of the torches. But they would have heard the single shot. The captain was prepared to waste some time in awaiting a reaction. Then, when his patience was exhausted, he would show some further interest in Edge and Luis Aviles.

'You think they will kill us, señor?'

Luis was persistent.

'After,' Edge answered shortly.

'After what?'

'The cat has played with the mice,' Edge replied and removed his hat. He squashed it up to form a pillow so that he would not have to rest his head on the stinking blanket, then stretched out on the bunk.

Luis, his eyes accustomed to the gloom now, looked on in amazement from his position crouched on the straw-littered floor.

'You can sleep at a time like this, señor?'

Long, even breathing and then a low snore was all the reply he received and after that, all he could do was sit and tremble in fear, listening to the silence and trying to estimate the passage of time when a second took a minute and a minute an hour. Eventually, he began to sob softly, recalling the old days when he had ridden with groups of bandits large enough to storm a fortress like Hoyos and wipe out every soldier there. Recalling, too, the ten thousand dollars, American. Money that he was certain he would now never see. Or would he? He brought his fear under control and tried to force his dull brain to think constructively. The tall American had asked him what value he placed upon his life, even though he did not believe the story of the ten thousand. Could he make the federal army captain believe him? Would the captain spare his life if he showed him where the money was hidden? A ray of hope stabbed through Luis' despair and he began to twist the crude ring around his finger, mind grinding out a plan of action that would save his life.

Edge, sleeping and yet not fully asleep, could hear the sounds made by Luis and was able to ignore them knowing they were not part of any threat. But when a series of sharp commands were voiced outside on the plaza and a door was thrown open, boots rapped on a hard floor, he came instantly awake.

'Señor,' Luis said in terror. 'They are coming for us.'

'And I'm going to ask the captain to cut out your tongue before he goes ahead with his own kind of tortures,' Edge replied evenly, just as the cell door burst open and light from a flaming torch showed four soldiers outside, perhaps the quartet that had escorted the prisoners there in the first place.

'You are to be interrogated,' one of them snapped. 'You will come with us. If you try to escape you will not be killed. But you will wish you were. On your feet.'

Luis leapt to his feet, while Edge took his time getting up from the bunk.

'Can I know the captain's name?' he asked, his voice as unhurried as his movements.

'Captain Jose Alfaro,' he was told. 'Why?'

Edge grinned coldly. 'I've an idea he ain't going to treat me nice. I want to know who to report to Abe Lincoln when I get back home.'

The soldier laughed shortly. 'You have been away too long, señor. Your president was shot dead at the theatre.'

Edge shrugged. 'Perils of politics,' he said and went to the door.

'I am a poor, honest Mexican,' Luis babbled as he followed.

'The Americano forced me to ride with him. Please tell Captain Alfaro of this.'

The short laugh again. 'The Captain has poor honest Mexicans for breakfast,' the soldier said.

'He save Americans for lunch?' Edge asked as he was urged forward by two rifle muzzles.

'No, señor,' the talkative soldier answered. 'Americans he puts through a grinder and sprinkles over the food for the dogs.'

They all laughed then, including the ingratiating Luis, who received a rifle butt against the back of his neck for his trouble. When they emerged into the plaza, Edge had to squint against the brightness of the light after the ink black of the cell. The torches were no longer held aloft by soldiers, but had been fixed into brackets jutting from building walls. And there were more torches than before, blazing bright enough to turn night into a close imitation of day. The soldiers now guarded the town of Hoyos from the top of the walls and the big wooden gates had been drawn closed. But Edge and Luis did not lack an audience as they were marched across the plaza towards a building hung with a sign: GOLDEN SUN CANTINA. For a large proportion of the civilian population of Hoyos had been encouraged from their homes by curiosity and had formed an expectant group across the junction where the town's main street led off the plaza. Neither of the prisoners paid attention to the many watching eyes, instead looked at a spot a few yards in front of the cantina door, where two soldiers had just completed digging a pair of holes, six feet apart, and were now hoisting poles into them.

'Señor,' Luis said nervously. 'Do you think what I think?'

Edge eyed the poles with dispassionate interest and clicked his tongue against his teeth.

The talkative soldier laughed harshly. 'I think the Americano knows we do not propose to fly flags of welcome,' he put in.

Luis began to pray, his voice low, the words tumbling from his lips at great speed. But the insistent prodding of rifle muzzles urged the prisoners between the poles and Luis curtailed his plea as he was thrust into the cantina. It was not a big

68

room, was probably one of many such bars in Hoyos. It had a long counter running down one side with a dozen or so chair flanked tables in the open area. Lighting was provided by evil-smelling oil lamps hung from the ceiling, their odour mingling with that of stale tequila, cooking fat, sawdust, vomit and rotting wood.

Captain Alfaro lounged behind a table at the rear of the room, drinking without enjoyment. On the table was a bottle of tequila from which he refilled his glass, and a heap of salt from which he took a pinch to place on the back of his hand before each sip. A thin column of smoke rose from the long cigar which rested on the edge of the table, the ash almost up to the wood. Edge and Luis were marched to within a yard of the table and ordered to halt. The soldiers backed off, levelling rifles. Alfaro, his dark, cruel eyes flicking from the face of Luis to that of Edge and back again, touched his tongue delicately to the salt, sipped the tequila. He did this three times before speaking.

'You are bandits.' It was not a question. Neither the voice nor the expression invited either agreement or disagreement. But Luis, his dull brain seething in a turmoil of fear, was unaware of such subtleties. He clasped his hands in front of his chest and his wizened face took on an ingratiating expression again, as the captain became suddenly more powerful than the Almighty.

'Oh no, my lord,' he said quickly, his voice a whine. 'I am a poor Mexican peasant escaping from the bandits. They attacked my village and killed all the people there. I am running from them.'

Alfaro licked and sipped, then pulled on his left ear lobe. Edge heard a movement behind and flicked a glance at Luis, saw the rifle butt slam into the Mexican's kidneys, saw his legs fold so that he went to his knees, heard the whoosh of escaping air.

'You will speak when ordered to do so,' Alfaro said coldly. 'I will give that order. You, too, gringo.'

The captain's eyes locked with those of Edge, who gazed back steadily, so that it was the other who broke, choosing to transwer his scorn to the more rewarding Luis. Luis, on his knees and therefore at a height disadvantage in relation to the seated captain, looked across the table like an apologetic dog.

'You are bandits,' Alfaro began again. 'You ride with the villain they call El Matador. I have excellent information that he and his band of cowardly dogs have been active north of Hoyos and now I await them. You were sent by El Matador to ensure that Hoyos would provide safe refuge. Speak.'

The salt and tequila ritual began again as the dark eyes looked with disinterest at the prisoners. Luis' mouth began to work, but he had trouble giving sound to the words.

'You're right,' Edge said evenly. 'El Matador and me are like that.' He crossed his second finger over his first and held up his hand, bringing it right back to his shoulder. Nobody made a move to stop him and he could easily have drawn the razor which still nestled undetected in its pouch. And he knew he could have slit the throat of the complacent captain. But in the next instant four bullets would have ripped into his back. Edge dropped his hand. 'Down at the foot of the trail there is a group of one hundred men. I figure you haven't got long to live, Captain.'

'He lies, he lies!' Luis screamed, finding his voice at last, having listened to Edge in open-mouth amazement.

Alfaro ignored Luis, watching Edge. 'I believe some of what you say,' he said. 'That you ride with El Matador. Perhaps that he and his men are waiting below. But not one hundred, Americano. I told you my information is reliable and I know there are not more than twenty-five of the pigs in the band.'

'It is right,' Luis agreed, nodding his head violently. 'That is how many rode into my village of San Murias and killed all the people.'

Alfaro nodded and sighed, turned to Luis with a show of patient reluctance. Then his eyes shot fire at the kneeling man. 'If you are a poor, honest peasant as you claim, señor,' he said with deadly calm, 'why were you not killed with the rest? Why did El Matador spare your miserable carcase?'

'Captain, I hid . . . '

'Silence!' thundered Alfaro, and then turned to glower at

the unblinking Edge. 'Why did you confess so easily, Americano?'

Edge grinned icily. 'Figure we're two of a kind, captain. When we ask questions we like to get the answers we want to hear. We don't get them, we get mad. When I get mad, captain, somebody gets hurt. You got mad a while back and Luis here got hurt. So far, only my dignity has suffered.'

Captain Alfaro pasted a smile on to his handsome face. Then he grimaced as the smell of burning wood reached his nostrils. He picked up his cigar and drew against it, smiled again. 'It is even more undignified to be shot, gringo.'

'So shoot us,' Edge invited. 'I've told you what we are. It's your duty to execute us.'

'No!' Luis screamed. 'If he is a bandit, I am not, captain. I am a poor, honest . . .'

Alfaro had touched his earlobe again and this time the rifle butt cracked against Luis' skull, and the old man pitched sideways with a whimper, unconscious. The captain merely glanced at him, as if he were a sack of potatoes that had been knocked over. Then he returned his attention to Edge, eyes showing genuine interest in the man.

'Somebody who wants to die,' he muttered pensively, and drew deeply against the cigar. 'You are a new experience for me, señor.'

'I doubt it,' Edge answered.

'Señor?'

'You don't get to be an officer in the Mexican army without learning the techniques of torture,' Edge explained softly. 'You must have heard a hundred men plead with you to kill them.'

Alfaro smiled his understanding. 'Ah, I see. You think I will kill you anyway and so by telling me what you feel I wish to hear, you hope for an easy death?'

'Bright, as well as brutal,' Edge said with unconcealed sarcasm, his lips tightening into a fleeting line of satisfaction when he saw the anger leap into Alfaro's eyes.

'I am sorry to disappoint you, señor,' he snapped, lifted his glass to his lips, drank and then sent the glass flying across the cantina. It crashed into the wall and exploded splinters on to a nearby table. 'If you insult me, you insult my uniform, and my uniform represents El Presidente. Pick him up and prepare him for execution.'

This last was addressed to the soldiers as the captain stabbed a finger at the inert form of Luis. Two of them stepped forward, stooped and hauled the old man up by the armpits, dragged him towards the door. Alfaro jabbed his cigar into the heap of salt and it sizzled softly as the man rose to his feet.

'You,' he said, his eyes boring into Edge's face, 'will witness the death of your compadre before you discover just how much I have learned about the infliction of pain. So will you know to the full extent how tragically your plan has misfired.'

Edge did not flinch under the words and their accompanying stare, turned at the insistence of rifle muzzles and followed in the wake of the captain.

'Captain Alfaro,' he called softly.

The Mexican officer halted in the doorway and turned to look quizzically at Edge.

'Señor?'

'Doesn't Luis get a last request?'

Alfaro smiled. 'He could ask for nothing better than to be shot.'

Edge believed him.

CHAPTER TWELVE

THEY tied the limp body of Luis Aviles to the right-hand pole, with a rope at the ankles, waist and chest, fastening his hands behind his back. His unconscious head sagged forward so that his chin rested on his chest. The soldiers were brought down from the wall surrounding the town and while a firing squad of six was being selected Luis' two guards amused themselves by attempting to scale the old man's hat on to the top of the pole to which the condemned prisoner was bound. Those soldiers not actively engaged in the execution formed into a group on one side of the plaza, opposite the crowd of civilians who continued to watch in quiet acceptance of anything the captain decreed.

Edge stood between and slightly in front of his two guards, watching through narrowed lids as Alfaro strutted among his men, directing operations with little regard for formality. The spluttering torches were visibly losing their power as the pale grey of dawn streaked the sky.

The sombrero finally hitched on to the top of the pole and spun around several times to a huge cheer from the watching soldiers, and one of the two participants in the game tossed some coins to the other in settlement of a bet. The sudden burst of noise brought Luis back to consciousness and he shook his head several times to clear it, raised his eyes to look about him. Then his face contorted into a mask of fear as he realised his predicament.

'I am innocent!' he yelled, looking about wildly, his eyes stopping for a moment on the disinterested captain, then moving on to fasten on the impassive face of Edge. 'He lied. I am not a bandit. You will suffer the flames of hell for eternity if you kill an innocent man.'

Alfaro had lined up the firing squad, went through a parody

73

of an inspection of the six men, halting to flick a speck of dust from the shoulder of one, to fasten the button on the uniform of another. Then he stepped back, set fire to another cigar and spun on his heels to march over to where Edge stood.

'You are silent, señor,' he said. 'It will not be long before you are screaming like the old one. But you will be demanding death, not pleading for life.'

'In America,' Edge replied, 'we have a saying. Where there's life, there's hope. I have a little more hope than Luis.'

'Attention!' Captain Alfaro ordered and the firing squad dragged their feet together, straightened their shoulders.

'Captain!' Luis screamed as tears began to overflow his eyes. 'I have money. Much money. I can buy my life.'

'You are poor and honest,' Alfaro flung at the condemned man. 'Such people never have money.'

Luis shook his head in desperation. 'I am honest,' he screamed. 'Poor only because the money is not on me. But I can take you to it, captain. Ten thousand, American.'

The captain allowed a burst of laughter to rip from his lips and several of the soldiers shared his humour. On the other side of the plaza the watching townspeople did not join in the amusement. They looked on in sadness, neither knowing nor caring whether Luis was guilty of the crime for which he was being punished. But they felt a sympathy for the old man because he was one of them, a man at the mercy of a corrupt army, commanded in Hoyos by a brutal captain whose whim might just as easily have caused him to select any one of them in place of Luis. They, too, each of them knew, would have made wild claims in an effort to delay the crack of the rifles. So whether it be amusement or sympathy that was turned against Luis Aviles, it was based upon a common disbelief of the words he spoke.

In the whole plaza, only one man examined Luis with an expression which might indicate serious consideration of his words. That man was Edge, who until this point regarded the ten thousand dollars as a figment of a deranged imagination: a fantastic idea dreamed up by Luis to help him face his intolerable life as the poorest man among the destitute citizens of San Murias. But now Luis was pleading for his life, knew that even if

74

he were believed, he would have to fulfil the promise in order to avert his fate.

Captain Alfaro, still smiling his amusement, drew deeply against the cigar and raised his hand. Six rifles were raised in unison, levelled at the man tied to the pole, with its ridiculous adornment of the sombrero.

'The ring!' Luis screamed through his tears. 'My ring will lead you to my money.'

The fusillade came almost as a single sound which lashed across the plaza like a whip crack. Luis' head fell forward and his eyes grew enormously wide as he realised he could see the toes of his boots, that his poncho showed no blood-soaked holes and that he felt no pain. He raised his head in time to see the six man firing squad pitch forward, was filled with a tremendous surge of joy as he saw it was their blood which spouted to soak into the dust of the plaza.

With roars of panic the watching soldiers scattered, struggling to bring up their rifles, some loosing off wild shots at unseen targets as others fell and rolled, twisted and writhed as bullets ripped into vulnerable flesh. As one of the men guarding Edge collapsed into a heap with a bullet in his heart the other fought to recover from his shock, wasted too much time in the attempt. Edge moved with the speed of a desperate animal, the skill of a man who has learned his trade under the unrelenting eye of death itself.

His left arm snaked out and encircled the throat of the captain and he dragged him backwards as he turned to direct a kick at the guard, his boot crashing into a kneecap. The guard screamed and dropped his rifle as he went down, screamed again as Edge's right hand came clear of the back of his neck and flashed in an arc, the point of the razor slashing through the flesh of his throat. As the guard died Edge put his lips close to Captain Alfaro's ear.

'No gun,' he whispered as the captain fumbled with his buttoned holster flap, trying to get at his pistol. Struggling violently, the captain did not curtail his attempt, gasped as the razor sliced a great flap of flesh from the back of his hand. 'I said no gun,' Edge reminded. 'Adios, amigo. I figure you'll get a warm reception where you're going.'

He drew back his right hand and then drove it forward. Alfaro gave a gentle sigh as the razor stabbed neatly between his ribs and punctured a lung. Edge released his grip on the man's throat, let him fall and looked up to see who his benefactors were, as the shooting was halted abruptly by a sharp word of command. Edge saw Luis Aviles still tied to the pole, his body convulsed by the laughter of relief; the uniformed bodies of the soldiers spread across the plaza in many attitudes of sudden death; the frightened faces of the unharmed civilians as they got to their feet. And above all this, seeming to grow out of the hard adobe on top of the wall, the figures of a score of rifle-toting men, outlined starkly against the rapidly brightening sky. One of the men was almost comically shorter than the rest, and his weapon was not a rifle.

'I thought I killed you, gringo,' he called from his perch just to the right of the gate.

'I was lucky, I guess,' Edge replied, glancing down at a rifle dropped by one of the dead guards, estimating his chances.

El Matador laughed, the sound ringing out across the plaza. 'Not so lucky, I think, if we did not arrive. That Alfaro, he almost know as many ways to kill a man as me.'

Edge shrugged. 'Sometimes it's better to know how to live than how to kill.'

'Right,' El Matador agreed. 'Why they try to shoot him?' He gestured with his blunderbuss towards Luis, who had now recovered from his initial burst of joy, was listening to the exchange with fearful interest, suspecting that one threat had merely been replaced by another.

'Alfaro thought he was one of your men, scouting for you.'

Matador laughed once more. 'That quivering heap of skin and bone?' he snorted. 'I think I will carry out the execution so that all here may know that El Matador does not have such a shaking jellyfish in his band of brave men.'

'No, El Matador!' Luis pleaded. 'Please do not kill a poor, innocent peasant. I once was a . . .'

'Shut your stupid mouth,' Edge hissed at him as he moved over to the pole.

'What you doing, gringo?' El Matador demanded when he

saw the movement, failed to hear the words spoken between unmoving lips.

'Alfaro wasn't smart,' Edge called back. 'He wouldn't listen to Luis. Luis has a secret.'

'What is the secret?' The voice of the bandit was heavy with puzzled anger.

Edge looked around the plaza, at the bandits on the wall and the townspeople grouped at the head of the street. The examination was heavy with meaning.

'If we shout like this, it won't be a secret no more,' Edge said.

A low mumbling of discontent spread along the top of the wall.

'Silence,' El Matador commanded and launched himself forward, landed lightly on his feet. 'Cut the old man loose. We will talk.' He glanced up at his men. 'In private.'

Edge hurriedly slid the blood-stained razor back into its pouch, then stooped to take a knife from the body of a nearby soldier who no longer had a face, used its sharp blade to slice through the ropes binding Luis.

'I talk and you only open your mouth when you're spoken to,' he whispered close to Luis' ear. 'You're on borrowed time already, and death pays all debts.'

'Señor, anything you demand of me,' Luis said, coming away from the pole, staggering under the weight of his relief, as the bandits climbed down from the wall.

'You!' El Matador shouted at the citizens of Hoyos. 'My men need food, drink and rest. They have released you from the terror of the army. Make them welcome or you will wish that Captain Alfaro were still in command.'

The people broke into hurried movement to do the bandit chief's bidding, beckoning the bandits off the plaza and on to the street, into the houses and cantinas. Matador himself headed for the Golden Sun, just as the heavenly body for which it was named tipped the first rays of a new day over the horizon. He beckoned for a fat, heavy-breasted woman of thirty or so to follow him, then waved his heavy gun at Edge and Luis to do likewise.

'I pray for your success, señor,' Luis said in a hushed whisper as he fell in behind the swaying rump of the fat woman. 'El Matador, he is a very mean man.'

'Who spoke to you?' Edge demanded.

'Nobody señor,' the old man apologised hurriedly. 'A thousand pardons.'

'You'll need more than that to save your rotten hide.'

Luis did not speak for fear of Edge's anger, instead turned to give him a bewildered look.

'It'll cost you ten thousand, American,' Edge explained shortly.

The old man swallowed hard and entered the cantina as Matador began to berate the woman for her slowness, demanding she go to the kitchen and cook him a meal. He swaggered across to the table where Alfaro had carried out the interrogation, fell into the chair and grasped the almost empty bottle of tequila, tilted it to his lips without need of a glass or desire for salt. Edge folded his long body into a chair at an adjacent table while Luis stood uncomfortably between the two.

'More tequila, cow,' the bandit chief shouted, tossing aside the empty bottle and bringing the blunderbuss down with a crash on to the edge of the table. Its gaping muzzle pointed at Luis, who inched out of the line of fire.

Matador saw the movement and let out a burst of laughter as the woman padded out of the kitchen door, went behind the bar for a bottle and carried it over to the table. Edge thought she might have been pretty had her features not been enveloped in rolls of fat.

'I do not shoot a rich man until I know where his money is,' Matador said with a grin, snatching the bottle from the woman's pudgy hands, then releasing his gun to reach up and squeeze a large nipple clearly outlined under the black material of her dress. She winced with pain but made no sound, ambled back to the kitchen as the bandit thumped her hard on the rump, screaming: 'Food, cow.'

'She is much woman,' Luis tendered, with a sidelong look at Edge.

Matador grinned. 'You like her old man? Maybe if I like what you going to say, I give you her as well as your life.'

'Reckon that's worth ten thousand dollars, American,' Edge said softly.

The grin fell from Matador's face like a dropped veil and he snatched up the blunderbuss, pointed it at Edge. 'You no joke with me, señor,' he hissed. 'I got your life in my trigger finger. I squeeze and you dead. No mistake this time.'

'I never joke about money,' Edge answered.

Matador seemed to hold his breath for several moments. Then he nodded towards Luis. 'He has that much money?'

'He knows where it is,' Edge replied.

'I know where is ten thousand,' Matador said softly, still menacing the gun. 'A hundred thousand. In a bank at Mexico City.'

'This ain't in no bank,' Edge said, wondering idly if he was telling the truth. 'This is someplace we can get our hands on it. Easy.'

'Where is this place?'

Luis started to open his mouth, raise his right hand with the ring on the third finger. But then his lips clamped tight as Edge shot out a foot, kicking the old man hard on the shin. Edge grinned at Matador as Luis bent to massage his aching leg.

'That ain't no kind of a deal,' he said. 'Soon as you know, that, Hoyos ain't a healthy place for us no more. I got holes in my head to see out of, hear with and breathe through. I don't want any more.'

Matador's eyes glinted dangerously. 'Captain Alfaro was keeping you alive to maybe make you suffer a little, señor?' he asked softly.

'And I thought he just liked me,' Edge answered.

'I know more ways to make men suffer than he ever heard of.'

'Torture ain't reliable,' Edge said easily. 'Some men break early. Others take longer. Some men just die of plain fright. Better you let us take you where the money is.'

Matador eyed Luis. 'I think he break easy.'

Edge shook his head. 'No good. He knows the place. I know exactly where in that place.'

The kitchen door swung open and the woman padded out, carrying a plate piled high with tortillas. She slapped the plate down hard on the table before Matador, her eyes spitting hate at the top of his head.

'You live 'til we get to the place and you show me where,' the bandit said with finality, snatching up a tortilla and biting into it, his expression showing that the food met with his approval. 'Then I decide what to do with you. Hey, cow.'

The woman had begun to go back to the kitchen, turned with resignation to await another order from Matador. The bandit swung the blunderbuss, levelled it and squeezed the trigger. The vicious load peppered the woman's large breasts and she screamed, her hands going to the injured parts, blood oozing from between the clutching fingers. Then Matador drew one of his Colts and took careful aim as the woman's horror-filled eyes stared at him. The bullet drilled a neat hole in the centre of her forehead and she fell backwards, the skirts of her dress riding high up her naked thighs the flesh quivering with the death convulsion.

'It is a kind man who would put an injured cow out of her agony,' Matador said evenly, holstering his smoking revolver and picking up another tortilla.

'Why?' Luis gasped, unable to rip his eyes away from the thick, exposed flesh of the dead woman's legs.

'She would have been no good for you, amigo,' the bandit said. 'Those legs, they would have broke your back at the height of your passion. But it was not for that reason. This place, it is quiet. The cow may have heard our voices. As the Americano said, a secret is not a secret when others know of it.' He took a long drink with the new bottle, smacked his lips. 'Now I eat, then I sleep. After that we go and get the money.'

Edge rose to his feet, content with the situation as it stood. He jabbed a stiff finger into the ribs of Luis, dragging his fascinated gaze from the body of the dead woman.

'Come on, amigo,' he said wryly. 'Let's go find us some live ones.'

CHAPTER THIRTEEN

EDGE had too many other things on his mind to concern himself with the multitude of pleasures which the town of Hoyos had to offer a man. Primarily he wanted what he had come into Mexico for – the return of the money the bandits had stolen from him, and revenge against El Matador. But it did not take him long to decide that both these objectives would have to wait. For not all the bandits had accepted their leader's invitation to relax. Obviously following a standing order, two men lounged outside the cantina, their attitudes of ease made fraudulent by the watchful glints of their eyes. They were the fat Miguel and the pock-marked Torres and as Edge and Luis moved out of the doorway, Torres broke away from the other and started down the side of the cantina, obviously intent upon taking up sentry duty at the rear of the building.

'We going to find some girls?' Luis asked, eyes alight with excited anticipation as he headed towards the street entrance, from which came the sound of laughter and shouting, an occasional feminine scream which could have been of pain or delight.

Edge shook his head. 'I hope you find one that's got everything,' he said.

'Señor?' The wizened face was puckered with bewilderment.

'They ain't invented a pill for it yet.'

Luis grinned his understanding. 'A man's got to take chances, señor.'

Then he was gone, hurrying towards the sounds of gaiety. Edge nodded to Miguel and got no response, began to pick his way between the dead bodies of the soldiers, towards the centre of the plaza where their weapons had been heaped in an untidy pile. But he still had six feet to go when a rifle cracked and dust spurted up just ahead of him. He turned slowly to look back over his shoulder, saw Miguel with his repeater still raised to shoulder level, eye behind the backsight.

'Just looking,' Edge said.

'You are not a cat, señor,' the fat man said evenly. 'But curiosity, it can make you just as dead.'

Edge spat. 'And I ain't got but just the one life,' he said reflectively, spun and angled away from the heap of guns, going towards the building in which he and Luis had been held the night before. It was, in fact, a church, but it had been many years since it was used for religious purposes. It still had an altar with a crucifix fixed to the wall above and there were still two rows of pews with a central aisle dividing them. But the scarring of the wall above the altar told of shooting practice with the ornament as the target and a scattering of straw and filthy blankets on the pews and the floor between them indicated that the place served as a dormitory in times when Hoyos was overcrowded.

Edge took this all in with disinterest as he moved quickly down the aisle, went through a door to the right of the altar, found himself in what had been the priest's robing room. A door on the other side was locked, but the wooden hinges had rotted and fell away within moments as Edge prised at them with the dead soldier's knife. Outside he stood in a narrow space between the rear of the church and the wall of the town. The sun was well clear of the horizon now, but the area in which Edge stood – no wider than four feet – was in deep shadow. The wall was ten feet high at this point, sheer and smooth, offering no footholds. There was only one way up and Edge took it. He gritted his teeth, pressed his back against the rear of the church, swung one foot up against the town wall and began to push himself aloft.

As Edge was making his bid for escape, Luis Aviles was savouring a forthcoming delight, the like of which he had not experienced for more than forty years. He was leaning against a dresser in a room on the second floor of a bordello, watching with avid eyes as a girl of no more than fourteen began to unbutton a blouse which promised in its drape an upper body developed beyond her years. At first the girl had been terrified as Luis demanded her favours, his drooling mouth spitting words of terrible vengeance from El Matador if she did not go to a room with him.

The woman who ran the house was as fearful as the girl, certain that Luis' new-found freedom must indicate an agreement with the bandit chief. So she had dragged the girl up the stairs and into the room, warning her of an even more terrible ordeal should the anger of El Matador be turned against the house. But now the girl's fear of Luis had turned to disgust for him, her plain young face twisted into a sneer. 'You will not enjoy me, old man,' she hissed, fingers nimbly unfastening the buttons.

'If you are not good, I will ask El Matador to slice you up like a side of beef,' he returned, not seeing her expression, unable to take his eyes away from the firm swells of her breasts as each button came loose.

But then, just before the girl was about to pull the blouse wide, exhibit to Luis what lay on each side of the deep cleavage he could already see, the door burst open under the crash of a large boot and a drunken bandit swayed in the frame. His name was Alfredo and he was tall and broad enough to almost fill the doorway. His face was scarred and ugly behind the stubble of his beard and he had a twisted mouth and only one eye, the other gouged out in a knife fight. Luis gasped and thought he was the most fearsome man he had ever seen in his life.

'Ah, the *hombre* who came back from the dead,' he said gleefully, his lips curling back in an awful grin. 'First El Matador saved you from the soldiers and then something saved you from El Matador.'

Alfredo lumbered into the room as Luis flattened himself against the wall, as if seeking to become part of it, and the girl cringed on the bed, pulling her blouse around her. The bandit reached the bed in two strides, grasped the blouse and ripped it from the girl's body, laughed as the breasts came free, young, smooth and firm.

'This is what you want to see, *hombre*?' he demanded of Luis. 'The beautiful secrets of her body. Now you have your wish. I give her to you. But you must tell me your secret.' He shook his head, his single eye muzzy with too much tequila. 'A powerful secret to make El Matador spare your life.'

'I do not know . . .'

'El Matador is interested in one thing only,' Alfredo bore on. 'Money. You have told him where there is money. Lots of it, eh?'

'No, I . . .' Luis broke off again as the big bandit approached him, caught hold of his poncho in a bunched fist, lifted him and threw him bodily across the room, so that his body thudded on to that of the girl.

'El Matador, he always keep the money for himself. I, Alfredo, am tired of this. Tell me your powerful secret, *hombre*, or you die.'

As he finished speaking, Alfredo drew a revolver from its holster on each hip and levelled both weapons. Luis, breathing fast with fear, sweat releasing new odours from his filthy body, scrambled to the far side of the girl and cringed behind her. The bandit laughed and fired both guns, the bullets whining over the top of the shaking bodies to thud into the wall as the girl screamed and Luis whimpered.

'The money, *hombre*?' Alfredo demanded. 'Your secret, or take it to hell with you.'

'Tell him, stupid,' the girl cried, trying desperately to wriggle free of Luis' grip. But Luis found enormous strength in his terror and held her fast, an inadequate shield against the wrath of the big bandit. 'He will kill us both.'

'Do as she says,' Alfredo shouted and squeezed the triggers. Then again, and again. Six bullets skimmed across the bed, the rush of air seeming to get closer to the flesh at each report.

'Your secret!' Alfredo yelled in fury and loosed off the last two bullets from each gun, aiming lower, so that they all thudded into the bed in front of the girl's straining body, sending up a shower of feathers.

Snorting, the bandit hurled away the empty guns and moved towards the bed, drawing his knife. In the shooting and yelling nobody in the room had heard the thud of running footsteps on the stairs. Not until the thunderclap of the exploding blunderbuss filled the room, the oil lamp hung from the ceiling shattered and showered, did Alfredo halt his murderous movement. He turned his single eye towards the darkly glowering face of his leader and realisation hit him like a blow in the stomach. He dropped the knife with a clatter and fell to his knees, his hands clasped in supplication as his eye sent out a silent plea.

'I was joking, El Matador,' he croaked, all signs of his drunkenness gone. 'Having some fun with him and the girl.'

Matador's mouth set into a grim line, and his eyes glinted. 'And now we shall have some fun with you,' he said.

Edge had reached the top of the wall, was sweating freely from the exertion of the climb, his back and arms moving slowly, as if they were lead weights. He heard the gunfire from the house on the far side of the plaza and ignored it, thought it was probably part of some wild game with which the bandits were letting off steam. Here, in the hot shadows, it was quiet, only his own rasping breath disturbing the silence. At the end of his climb he rested, jammed ten feet above the ground with his back against the church and his feet planted firmly on to the wall. All he had to do now was drop his feet and push himself across the gap, hook his hands over the wall and haul himself up and over. But before he did this, he rested, closing his eyes against the bright sunlight, willing new strength into his arm muscles that would have to take the strain when he jumped.

'The gringo could hurt himself.'

Edge snapped open his eyes as a shadow fell across them and the soft words were spoken, found himself looking up at a bandit whose grinning face seemed a mile high as he stood upon the wall.

'I do this every morning,' Edge said with resignation. 'Exercise to keep me fit.'

'I think you are not so fit, señor,' the bandit replied and swung his rifle, upside down, so that the butt crashed with force into the side of Edge's legs.

Edge's feet came away from the wall and he plunged to the ground, landed with a thud on his back to lay gasping for breath.

'No, not so fit,' the bandit said with a laugh. 'Maybe you should sake such exercise in the afternoon as well.'

Edge cursed softly as the bandit continued his patrol of the top of the wall. But the man paid him no heed, found something

85

down in the plaza which was a greater source of interest than a bruised and breathless Americano. What he could see was a group of bandits, led by the tiny El Matador, dragging the unfortunate Alfredo from the street into the wide plaza. The one-eyed man was screaming his innocence, the words barely understandable through his racking sobs, and falling upon unheeding ears. His hands were tied together in front of him, the loose length of the rope held by other bandits. When the group reached the edge of the plaza, El Matador went to lean against the wall of the Golden Sun Cantina and at a nod of his head the bandits broke into a fast run, shouting and cheering in drunken glee. Forced to join them, his hands jerked out in front of him, Alfredo found it impossible to retain his balance. So that as the bandits went into a turn at the corner of the plaza, the prisoner stumbled and pitched forward, to be dragged full length over the rough, sun-hardened surface. The bandits completed two circuits of the plaza, their pace slowing and their ebullience faltering as sun and drink took toll on out-of-condition bodies. But the run had been long enough to tear through the clothes and flesh of the wretched Alfredo, who was hauled erect to exhibit a sickening sight of blood, dust and tattered clothing from chest to knee. His face, too, was lacerated at forehead and jaw where his head had bounced on the hard ground.

Unable to offer resistance, Alfredo stood in meek supplication before El Matador, blinking his single eye and awaiting sentence.

'We are a band of men,' the tiny leader told him, having to raise his head to look up into the bloodied face. 'As your chief, I must sometimes act alone. You are not chief, Alfredo.'

Alfredo's mouth worked, but no words fell from his lips. Matador gave him only a moment, then pointed to the two poles which had been erected for the execution of Edge and Luis.

'Between them,' Matador instructed. 'Then get the biggest and the bravest.'

Minutes later, when Edge emerged from the church, it was to see the big Alfredo spread-eagled between the poles, arms held high and wide by ropes hitched at the top, legs pulled into an opposite splay with ropes tied at the bottom. The only other figure in the plaza was that of El Matador who stood in front of and slightly to the left of the poles, hands held behind his back. Edge was puzzled by the scene, then noticed that most of the other bandits had climbed up on to the wall from which they had made their attack earlier. But not all. Miguel was not among them, and when he did appear it was astride a horse, riding fast down the street, wheeling into the plaza as if death itself was on his heels.

And in a way it was, for thundering into the square behind him came an enormous black bull, snorting through his running nostrils and slapping his tail angrily. The enraged beast followed horse and rider in a wide arc across the plaza to the accompaniment of a huge cheer from the watching bandits. Then Miguel reined his mount into a tight turn and the lumbering bull bellowed his rage as forward momentum carried him past. When he finally halted, his flank slamming into the wall, it was to see horse and fat rider disappearing down the street on the other side of the plaza. As the hoofbeats died, silence descended, for the bandits high above the scene had lapsed into quiet expectation.

Then: 'Hi, toro!'

The red eyes of the bull flicked to the source of the sound, saw the tiny figure of El Matador stride to the centre of the plaza, bringing forward his hands and unfurling a red cape. The beast snorted and beat on the ground with a front hoof.

Alfredo whimpered.

'Toro! Toro!'

El Matador raised his voice and stamped his heels. The bull bellowed, lowered his head and charged, the vicious points of his massive horns flashing in the sunlight, hoofs thundering on the ground and resounding between the façades of the buildings facing the plaza.

The bandit chief was skilful in his art, making a graceful pass, having to go up on to his toes to get the height with which to take the cape clear of the horns. Then, as the animal bellowed in a rage of frustration, Matador ran to his former position and all who watched could see the soundless working of Alfredo's lips. The bull came about in a lumbering turn and stood pawing the ground once more, searching for a target. Bandits cheered.

'Hi, toro!'

Silence.

The ugly head went down and hoofs thudded. Horns moved from side to side with evil menace as, grinning coldly, Matador raised the cape so that it covered the area of Alfredo's stomach. The man who was to die watched with his single eye wide, his mouth gaping in a silent scream that did not erupt into sound until his final moment of life. Timing his move to perfection, Matador jumped to the side with great agility, letting go of the cape. The bull, maddened by the sudden darkness of the blindfold shook his head to try to escape. And at that instant one of his horns gored into Alfredo's lower stomach, the head movement twisting the needle sharp point into the man's entrails. The speed and force of the charge tore the screaming Alfredo free, ripping his arms from his sockets and snapping the ropes at his feet. Then, as the massive beast skidded to a halt, he tossed his head and the body of the man sailed skywards, cartwheeled and thudded to death, head first.

'Toro!'

The stunned silence was broken by the single word of taunt and the bull, intent upon his victim, saw a movement and lowered his head to make a charge.

'Unorthodox,' Edge muttered from the doorway of the church.

Instead of a sword, Matador had supported the cape with a rifle and now as he stood in the path of the charging bull he raised it with a cool grace, pulled back the hammer and waited.

CRACK.

The heavy calibre bullet found the precise spot where a true matador would have placed the sword at the moment of truth: and the animal fell in its tracks without making a sound. Edge looked up at the bandits on the wall and grinned icily.

'Figure we got beef steak for lunch,' he said.

CHAPTER FOURTEEN

THEY rode out at mid-afternoon, El Matador leading the way down the narrow trail from Hoyos. Miguel and Torres followed him and behind were Edge and Luis, with the other bandits taking up single file position at the rear. Luis was in a particularly good mood. He had spent the day with the teenage girl of his choice and had been given Alfredo's horse to ride after pointing out to Matador that his burro would slow down the journey south towards the money. He was a man who lived for the moment and as the group reached the foot of the plateau and the pace quickened, Luis felt good: rested, well fed, satiated with sex, riding a good horse with a vicious band of desperadoes. It was like the old days and he almost felt young again.

But there was no such mood of contentment upon Edge. He was thinking of what lay ahead, his mind concerned with the ten thousand dollars and the doubt of its existence. And if it did exist, would the old man be able to find it. If he did find it, how to escape death. For there was one factor in the future about which Edge had no doubt: that the bandit chief intended both Edge and Luis Aviles to die. And the tall, lean American had only his razor with which to make a play, Matador having disarmed him of the knife before they set out from Hoyos.

So as the group rode through the hot afternoon and into the cold of the night, Edge's expression was set into lines of deep thought. Matador did not appear to notice this, or perhaps chose to ignore it in his confidence of dealing with any situation as it arose. For the most part he himself rode in silence, only occasionally turning in the saddle to ask Luis how much further. And each time he got the same response:

'Some way, El Matador. I will tell you.'

The men of the group who at first had shared the good mood

of Luis, their demeanour arising out of their own sense of well being, became noticeably less enthusiastic as the tiring ride took its toll of their good spirits. And there were murmurings of discontent, this new mood created by the realisation that they did not know where they were going, or why. That was a secret shared only by El Matador, Luis Aviles and the Americano. But they were persuaded to accept the fact of such a secret by the memory of what had befallen Alfredo when he attempted to discover it.

It was Miguel's horse that was shot from under him and a bandit named Juan who was blinded by a bullet creasing across one eye and smashing through the bridge of his nose to gouge out the other. The group was riding below a ridge and the fusillade of shots came from the high ground. It was followed closely by another as the white clad men slid hurriedly from their saddles and dived behind a scattering of rocks, shouting their shocked surprise and firing blindly.

Edge found himself sharing cover with the terrified Luis, grimaced as this new fear aroused a fresh wave of evil odour from the old man's body. 'Your pa must have been a polecat,' he muttered with distaste.

'Pardon, señor,' Luis answered. 'I think I have an accident.'

'That's all I need,' Edge said and waited for a lull in the shooting, made a dash for another rock and threw himself behind it as a bullet tugged at his sleeve.

He found himself stretched out beside El Matador. 'Hell, the whole thing stinks,' he murmured.

The bandit chief ignored him, looked around the rock to where the blinded Juan was stumbling about, holding blood soaked hands to his face, screaming for help. Matador raised his Colt and shot the man in the back, ending the noise.

'That Juan, he always had trouble with his eyes,' Matador hissed. 'I think he cured now.'

'Surrender in the name of El Presidente!' a voice called from above. 'This is Colonel Adame of the Mexican Republican Army. I have a warrant for your arrest, El Matador.'

'He talks a lot, does he not?' Matador said to Edge.

Edge looked to left and right, at the bandits sheltering behind protective rocks. 'He don't only talk,' he answered.

El Matador spat and looked to his right. 'Hey, Miguel.'

The fat bandit with the ring in his ear gave an answering grunt.

'We do like at Rosario, amigo.'

Miguel's teeth flashed in a grin and he turned to pass the word along the line. Torres sent the message in the other direction.

'Colonel!' Matador called. 'Five of our number are dead. We will surrender.'

There was a moment's pause. Then: 'Stand, with arms above the head.'

Matador lay his blunderbuss against the rock and dug Edge in the ribs as he got to his feet. 'You are not among the five, señor.'

Edge sighed and hauled himself up beside the tiny bandit, glanced to left and right and saw the majority of the other bandits do likewise, resting rifles against the rocks and raising their hands high. Five men, including Miguel and Torres, remained flat on the ground. Up on the ridge stones rattled underfoot as the soldiers came from behind their cover and started down. Edge counted ten of them, clearly visible in the pale moonlight that showed them up as solid black against the bleached rock.

'You will all move forward,' the officer instructed as the buttons of his uniform glinted in the light.

The bandits did so, going around to the front of the rocks.

'I am not one of these . . . ' Luis started to blurt out, snapped his mouth shut as a bullet chipped splinters from the rock behind him.

'Silence,' the colonel yelled, leading his men down, holding a revolver out in front of him. The men carried rifles.

'Colonel, my ear itches,' Matador said in a conversational tone as the soldiers reached the foot of the ridge.

Even as he spoke, the bandit chief lowered his arm and his fingers tugged at his right earlobe. Edge saw the signal and was turning before the first shot rang out. He was hidden behind the rock and looking with hooded eyes from safety before the first five soldiers had even hit the ground. Two of the bandits who had played possum went down under the return of fire and one other who was not fast enough in grabbing his rifle and diving for cover, died with three bullets in his heart. Two more soldiers died as they turned to run, two more as they stood their ground. Colonel Adame caught the full blast of El Matador's weapon in the stomach before two rifle bullets in the head ended his agony. Incredibly Luis Aviles, who had been rooted by fear to his exposed position, did not even get scratched by a splinter of blasted rock.

Matador looked along the line of bandits as they stood and made a sound of disgust. 'We are getting slow,' he said. 'At Rosario we lost only one and there were fifteen pigs of soldiers.'

'It was only they who were slow,' Torres said resentfully, pointing to the three dead bandits.

The truth of the comment did not lighten the little chief's mood. 'Round up the horses,' he ordered curtly, and glowered at Luis. 'How far now, jellyfish?'

'Some way, El Matador,' the old man answered as before, his voice trembling. 'I will tell you.'

Matador spat and sat on a rock to await the carrying out of his order. It took a considerable time, for the loose horses of the bandits had bolted at the sound of gunfire and there were not enough of the soldier's mounts to go around. But some of the spooked animals were captured and Edge was as relieved as Matador to see that the chief's mount was among them. The bulging saddlebags on the big white stallion revealed the new resting place for the money taken from the Peaceville bank and sheriff's office.

But when the animals were counted and assigned, the group was still one horse short. Luis Aviles, standing meekly beside the rock, still recovering from his fear, was the man without a mount. The bandits, high in their saddles, refused to meet his imploring eyes, each fearing he would be elected to carry a foul smelling passenger. But, as he prepared to mount, Matador heard a groan from one of the soldiers and moved quickly to the side of the prone figure, drawing a knife. He stopped and flipped the man over on to his back, evil eyes searching for a wound. But there was only a tiny trickle of blood from a graze on the man's brow where a bullet had creased the skin, stunning him. A diabolical grin spread across Matador's face.

'I think we have an animal for our amigo to ride,' he called. 'Not a horse, but a beggar cannot be a chooser as the gringos say.' He hauled the dazed man to his feet. 'A pig, he will do, I think.'

The soldier was young. A recently appointed corporal, the freshness of his insignia evidencing the short period of his new rank. He was tall, towering over the tiny figure of Matador. But his fear as he became aware of the menacing expressions of the surrounding bandits seemed to reduce him in stature. Matador placed his blunderbuss stock into the small of the man's back and shoved him forward. As he stumbled to a halt before Luis Aviles, the old man's grizzled features broke once more into a smile. There was another, more humiliated than himself and his ego became inflated as a direct result.

'I am a skilled rider of pigs,' Luis said gleefully and made a circling gesture with a finger, instructing the corporal, to turn round. Then he leapt upon the man's back, hooking his arms around the soldier's neck, legs around his middle. 'Look, I ride him bareback.'

The bandits burst into raucous laughter and heeled their horses forward as Matador mounted and went out in front, beckoned for the soldier to trot ahead of him.

Matador kept the pace at a walk for several minutes and the only sounds were the mocking words of encouragement from Luis and the weary breathing of the man to whose back he clung. Riding in the centre of the group, Edge realised that time was running out fast for the corporal. As sport, the sight of a man acting as a horse had quickly lost its novelty and the only one who continued to enjoy the circumstances was Luis.

'Your pig is slow,' Matador said suddenly. 'Can you not get more speed from him?'

The soldier's ragged breathing was suddenly interrupted by a gasp as Luis brought his heel down hard against the man's stomach. The soldier broke into a run, weaving from side to side, chin banging on his chest. Luis was small, weighed little, but with each step the burden became heavier. Abruptly, a cramp stabbed at the soldier's leg and he pitched forward, hurling Luis over his head. Luis landed with a cry of alarm as the soldier curled into a foetal position, fingers clawing at the pain in his leg. Matador reined in his horse and slid from the saddle. He stooped over the soldier who cowered beneath him, face twisted by pain.

'I think you broke your leg,' Matador whispered. 'Pigs are like horses and we are kind to them. A broken leg, it is no good to any beast.'

He swivelled his holster and fired the Colt through the opening at the bottom, the merciful bullet smashing through the skull and into the brain. Matador straightened with a sigh and looked around, seeing they were in the moon shade of a bluff, that a stand of yuccas was at hand to provide fuel for a fire.

'How far now, amigo?' he asked Luis as the old man got painfully to his feet.

Luis looked to the south. 'Not far now, El Matador,' he said. 'Soon I will tell you.'

The bandit chief nodded. 'We make camp here.' Then he looked at Edge, recalling the tall man's comment when he had killed the bull. He grinned and glanced at the dead soldier. 'You want pork for supper, señor?'

Edge spat. 'Obliged, but there ain't no R in the month,' he answered.

CHAPTER FIFTEEN

AT sunup the next morning Edge came awake to see the bandits in a huddle, whispering angrily among themselves as El Matador held his peace in the centre of the group. Edge did not move but continued to watch and wait for developments. The camp had been made at the very foot of the bluff and Edge and Luis Aviles were still stretched out under blankets in the deep shade, feet towards the powdered remains of the fire that had kept back the cold during the night. The bandits were several yards away, catching the first warmth of the new day, so that their many-sided conversation which was carried out in tones of low anger reached Edge as just a murmur. He had a strong idea that they were not keeping down their voices for the benefit of the two apparent sleepers.

'All right,' El Matador said at length when his patience was exhausted and he had picked up sufficient of the gist of his men's complaints. He stood up. 'I will ask.'

The bandits made sounds of satisfaction and also got noisily to their feet, so that Edge was able to use these sounds as a pretence for waking. And as he sat up and watched the approach of the group he saw their expressions bore out his judgement of their previous tone. They were angry to the point of collective ugliness and presented a menacing prospect: the bullets slotted into bandoliers glinting in the early sunlight, their eyes flashing in the shadows of sombreros and a threat of death was in every one of their many weapons.

'Guess you ain't come to offer me breakfast?' Edge said, tossing off the blanket and getting to his feet.

'I wish to know when we will reach our destination, señor,' Matador said coldly, and the men at his back nodded to indicate this had been a collective decision.

Edge moved his tongue, trying to dislodge a piece of meat

trapped between two teeth. 'You want to speak to my amigo,' he said, stooped to pick up a rock and tossed it towards the still sleeping form of Luis Aviles. The missile hit without force, but the old man yelled as if from great pain and sat up with a show of injury. 'Time to answer the ten thousand dollar question,' Edge said, ignoring the dangerous flash of Matador's eyes. It was obvious the little chief had still not told his men of their objective.

'It is a manner of the Americano's speech,' Matador said hurriedly, stepping forward to stand over Luis. 'How far?'

The question was lashed out and Luis winced just as if a whip had stung him. 'I said last night,' the old man answered quickly. 'Not far now, El Matador.'

'Today?'

Luis shrugged, looking miserable. 'Perhaps, if we ride fast.'

Matador nodded and spun on his heels to glower at his men. 'We ride fast, no?'

The bandits made a token show of consulting one another, whispering among themselves. Then they all nodded but without enthusiasm.

'When we get there, you will see our ride has been worthwhile,' Matador tossed at them, but the group broke up and went across to saddle their horses without responding to their leader's remark. The little man spat angrily and stooped low over the cowering Luis. 'Old man,' he said, cold and low. 'My men are restless and tired of this journey. If we do not reach the end of it before noon, I will cut off that which makes you a man and push it down your throat so that it chokes you.'

Luis looked at Edge, found the tall American grinning at him, offering no comfort. 'I think I'll skip lunch,' he said.

Matador suddenly laughed harshly. 'Hey, I think maybe I have to think of something else. Such a small thing would not fill such a big mouth.'

Still laughing, he turned and strode away towards his horse.

'Señor,' Luis said plaintively, and Edge looked at him. 'I do not think we can get there when he says.'

Edge shrugged. 'Tough.'

He went to saddle his horse and Luis to find a partner

so that it was not many minutes before the group was on the move again, continuing to strike south, taking advantage of the coolness of early morning to make good time. But as the sun hauled itself higher to burn down with a merciless disregard for human and animal life, the pace slowed. Men and horses sweated freely and there was precious little shade for the group while it continued to move. Matador was again in the lead, but now Luis rode beside him and as they made slow progress through a deep arroyo Edge, immediately behind the leaders, could hear their conversation.

'How you know about this money?' the bandit chief demanded.

'I was one of them that stole it,' Luis answered and there was a note of pride in his reedy voice. Once again his dull mind had forgotten the threat that hung over his life. Now he was not only riding in a bandit group, but was alongside the leader at the head of the column, mounted behind Miguel.

'You really were a bandit?' Matador asked in a tone of disbelief.

Luis nodded. 'Many years ago. We were the most feared band in all Mexico. We killed many, stole much.'

'Where this ten thousand, American come from?'

'From a stage, El Matador,' came the reply. 'In Texas in the United States of America. Our chief led us in an attack on a stage carrying the payroll from San Antonio to an army fort on the Rio Grande del Norte, El Matador. There were soldiers guarding the stage and we lost many men. But we killed all of them.' The old man smacked his lips at the memory of the carnage.

'And what was left of you rode south?'

'Yes, El Matador. We rode hard and fast for the word spread about our great feat. There were many other bandits who thought they could take the money from us. And Indians, too, El Matador. The theft made us famous. We killed hundreds – thousands – as we rode south. And we lost many more, until there were just three of us left.'

'So you hid the money?'

'That is right.' His tone became secretive and Edge had to strain forward in his saddle to pick up Luis' words. 'At night we hid it in a safe place and were to wait until the time was right. But we were betrayed. One of us was killed when they came for us and another died in the prison in Mexico City. Only I survived to know the hiding place. But I was in the prison for many long years.' He tapped a finger at the side of his head. 'My mind, it suffered as well as my body from the beatings I was given. Sometimes I do not remember too good, El Matador.'

'But you remember now,' Matador said, his voice suddenly loud in its harshness.

'Oh yes,' Luis came back quickly. 'Now I not forget. I went north when I was released. I knew it was in the north we held up the stage. But I found the village of San Murias . . . ' He shrugged. 'Time went by. I was getting old and often it seemed too troublesome to make another long journey. But then, El Matador, I see what you did at San Murias. I recall the old days when I was like you, and I remember the place.'

Matador nodded and grunted with satisfaction. Suddenly he slid his foot from the stirrup and raised his leg, kicked sideways. The toe of his boot found Luis' rib cage and the old man went out off the horse with a cry of alarm and thudded to the ground. Edge heard a series of clicks behind him and knew that more than a dozen rifles were trained upon his back, anxious fingers curled around sensitive triggers. He halted his horse and watched through hooded eyes as Matador stood over the old man, aiming the Turkish scattergun.

'It is noon,' the bandit chief said coldly. 'Time has run out for you, amigo.'

Every muscle in the old man's body had begun to tremble and saliva was bubbling out of the corners of his mouth to trickle down into his beard. Although he was not close enough to catch the scent, Edge wrinkled his nostrils as his imagination created the stink that would be rising from the quivering flesh. He turned his attention to the bulging saddlebags on the horse ahead, figuring his chances. A glance over his shoulder at the concerted menace of the bandits told him the odds were long enough to verge upon the impossible.

'Hey, gringo!' El Matador called, and captured the American's attention. 'I think your amigo is cold, he shivers so much.

It would be good for him to sunbathe a little, I think.'

Edge sighed and slid from the saddle.

'Miguel, the pegs.'

The fat bandit with the ring in his ear delved into his saddle-bag and came out with four iron pegs, tossed them to the feet of Edge.

'To sunbathe with the clothes on is not so healthful,' El Matador was muttering to Luis. 'You will disrobe, amigo. Then lay on the ground thus.'

The tiny bandit spread his legs apart and raised his hands above his head.

'El Matador!' Luis pleaded, the words bubbling in his throat.

A crack across the head from the blunderbuss put a full stop to the entreaty.

'If you do not remove your clothes, I will do it for you. I will cut them from you and I too am cold. My hand may shake.'

Matador laughed as Luis' trembling fingers tore at the buttons of his shirt. During this exchange Miguel had unhooked a lariat from his saddle horn and had cut four pieces of rope about twelve inches long. These he tossed on top of the pegs.

'This ain't something you just thought up then?' Edge asked softly.

Miguel grinned, his bulbous features taking on many new rolls of flesh. 'There is nothing new under the sun, señor,' he said.

Luis, menaced into silence by the threat of Matador's face, took off his final garment to expose the full nakedness of his frail body to the heat of the blazing sun.

'Down!' he was ordered and he sat and then stretched out full length, wincing as the burning hardness of the ground touched his bare flesh.

'Gringo!'

Edge drove in the pegs, using the heel of his boot to hammer them into the unyielding earth, then tied the lengths of rope around the bare wrists and ankles, hitched the ends to the pegs. Matador had gone with the others, leading the horses into a patch of shade from a stand of yuccas, and Edge was able to talk to Luis without being overheard.

'Sorry about this, amigo,' he said softly, hardly moving his lips, and with no sincerity in the words.

There were tears in the old man's eyes, perhaps of regret, perhaps because the sun was already making its heat felt on his vulnerable, crinkled flesh. 'I will not tell them,' he said and the vehemence of his tone caused Edge to glance at his face. He saw that, despite the moisture in the eyes, the old man's face was set into an expression of grim determination. Edge could see in the face, behind the wizened lines of age, something of the character of Luis Aviles in his heyday. He had been tough and mean and as brave as any other. But life had dealt him too many blows, pummelling the strength out of him. But while he lacked his former physical potency, there was still, below the surface of his weakness, a reserve of stamina which now fed his resolve to outwit the evil El Matador.

'Luis,' Edge said softly.

'Señor?'

'Is there ten thousand, American?'

'There is, señor,' the old man said. 'You have saved my life many times for either the soldiers or El Matador would have killed me before this had you not been with me. You did not do these things for me, I know. But no matter. The money is in the town of Montijo, not ten miles south of this place. Much good will it do you, but my ring provides the key to the hiding place.'

Edge glanced at the third finger on the right hand of Luis Aviles, but could ask no further questions as a shadow fell across him and he looked up to see Matador standing over him. The bandit chief stooped to test each knot, nodded his satisfaction at their security.

'You did well, gringo,' he said, gesturing with the blunderbuss. 'Come, join us in the shade to drink some cool water. We will return in an hour to see the healthful effect of the sun upon our compadre.'

It was high noon now and the lips of the old man were already beginning to crust with sunburn. But he made no further plea for mercy and his expression as he returned the evil grin of the bandit chief was one of iron determination. Edge saw Matador's expression darken at this new side of Luis' character. But then the blunderbuss came up and Edge moved across to where the bandits waited, lounging in the tree shade, sucking at the necks of their water canteens. But there were no canteens on Edge's horse and he was not offered a drink by any of the men.

They sat for perhaps thirty minutes, talking idly amongst themselves at first, but then lapsing into silence. All but one completely ignored Edge, who was concentrating his attention upon Luis Aviles as the old man suffered out in the baking sun. But the American was aware of the interest of the pock-marked Torres and of the way he continually fingered the knife at his waist. Finally, the disease-scarred bandit spoke.

'El Matador?'

The bandit chief had been dozing, face hidden by the tilt of his sombrero. But he came awake at his name and pushed up the brim, looked questioningly at Torres.

'It is a long time since I have practised with my knife. I am fearful my skill will grow less from neglect.'

The other bandits were suddenly alive with interest, antici-pating some entertainment to break the monotony of the wait. Matador saw the focus of Torres' attention and his dark eyes locked upon those of Edge. The familiar evil grin spread across his young face.

'I am not sure that the Americano knows that which he says he knows,' the chief said slowly. 'But we must keep him alive in case he does – and the old man fries to his death.'

'Obliged,' Edge said.

'But,' Matador continued. 'You are right, Torres. You are our most skilled fighter with the knife and your art is most valuable to us.' His grin broadened. 'You may cut him as many times as you like, but he must not die. If he does, you will die, too.' He patted the stock of his blunderbuss. 'There are other knife fighters in Mexico.'

Edge looked back at Torres, saw from the smile on the man's face that he did not fear for his life. He was confident that his skill could reduce Edge to a bloody pulp without causing his opponent to die. Torres drew his knife, a long bladed dagger, honed on both sides and needle sharp at the point.

'What about me?' Edge asked, snapping a quick glance at Matador.

'It is a pity,' the bandit chief said with a shrug. 'But we cannot spare another weapon for you. Try not to get too cut up about it.'

As the bandits laughed at the joke, Torres leapt to his feet and lunged. Edge went sideways fast, springing to his feet.

'A real sharp character,' he muttered as the blade flashed by his head.

'You'll get the point,' Matador laughed.

CHAPTER SIXTEEN

EDGE'S lithe body weaved from side to side and his feet danced with amazing agility at each lunge of the bandit Torres. At first the scarred face had been wreathed in a smile, his teeth and eyes flashing as brightly as the polished blade of his knife. But it did not take him many seconds to realise the defensive skill of his adversary and his expression darkened with his awareness. Edge did not smile: his eyes glinted from between narrowed lids, ever watchful for a sign to betray the next move of the man with the knife and his lips were mostly set in a straight, firm line only splitting open to gulp in a fresh supply of air upon each occasion he evaded the lunge of the weapon. The watching bandits, too, underwent an abrupt change of mood. At first they had yelled ecstatic encouragement to Torres, anticipating a spurt of red blood to announce the completion of each thrust. But, as time and time again the lean, hard body parried the attack they started to chide their fellow bandit, tossing out insults to his skill with a knife.

Edge, his face showing no sign of what he was thinking, welcomed the altered attitude of the watchers. For Torres, already angry at his own failure to make an early strike, was pushed deeper into his rage by the epithets thrown at him. He began to curse softly under his breath and his lunges became more frequent so that his timing went awry and nine out of ten of the thrusts were such that Edge could avoid them with complete ease. The man's breathing became ragged and as Edge drew the fight out of the shadow, into the hard brightness of the sun, Torres began to sweat freely, had often to raise a hand and brush the stinging salt from his eyes.

The watching bandits moved with the fight, forming a circle around the two participants, leaving their rifles behind. Again Edge's expression gave no sign that this move meshed in with his plan of campaign and to the watchers it seemed that his complete attention was focussed upon Torres, his mind fully engaged with measures to avoid the flashing blade. If any had known Edge better, they may have suspected such an assumption was incorrect when the American let his eyes rest upon the figure of Matador a fraction of a second too long, and received a shallow gash on his forearm as punishment. But the bandits merely shouted with glee at this first sight of blood and again began to yell in favour of Torres.

Edge considered the wound a fair price, for he had seen that Matador was in position, two yards to his left and not more than six yards from where the horses were hobbled.

He sidestepped once, twice, placing himself within inches of the tiny bandit chief. Torres lunged and Edge brought up his foot. The knife nicked into the flesh of Edge's shoulder, then fell from nerveless fingers as a toecap found Torres' groin. The man yelled in agony and doubled up, hands flying to his injured part. Matador stepped to Edge's right so that he could see around the big man and Edge leapt into a backwards movement, right hand flashing to his neck.

Matador was quick to sense danger, but not quick enough in taking avoiding action. Before he had even started to reach for his guns Edge had grasped him around the chest, pinning one arm to his side, and raised the open razor to press against the pulsing neck.

'Anyone makes a move, El Matador meets his moment of truth.'

It was suddenly deathly quiet. Even Torres, still doubled up in his agony, ceased his groaning to look up at Edge and his prisoner. Like the other bandits in the ragged circle, he was aghast at what had happened, amazed by the speed of the turnabout.

'Do as he says,' Matador said, no trace of fear in his voice.

They obeyed and Edge let out his breath in a silent sigh. El Matador was not a popular leader and any of the bandits could have grasped this opportunity to be rid of him. But the little man had ruled with a rod of iron and countless memories of his wrath had a cowering effect on the men. The little chief had led a charmed life and in a shoot out might still survive to return and reap vengeance upon any man who did not bow to his wish.

'I give you your freedom, gringo,' Matador said evenly to Edge.

'Obliged,' Edge said, and lifted the tiny man easily from the ground with the arm around his chest while maintaining the pressure of the razor against his throat.

'You keep the razor in a good place,' Matador congratulated as Edge backed away, keeping the chief's body between himself and the other bandits. 'I will kill the man who searched you for weapons.'

'You're optimistic,' Edge told him as he bumped into the flank of a horse, flicked a glance to left and right, spotted Matador's stallion and sidled over to it. He kicked the hobble free. 'Open the saddlebag, amigo.'

For the first time, he felt the bandit's body suffer a tremor. The man apparently valued money more than he did his life.

'We ride together, señor,' he said, and even his voice had a quiver. 'We split the money. Also the ten thousand, American.'

Edge applied pressure to the razor, drew a droplet of blood. Life became the more precious and Matador used his free hand to unfasten the catch. It was not easy and his hand moved awkwardly as his feet dangled some twelve inches from the ground. His men watched with bewilderment replacing their stunned anger. The flap came free and as it did so, three one dollar bills fluttered to the ground. Several of the watching bandits licked their lips and shuffled their feet.

'Obliged,' Edge said and moved the razor, drawing it in a hard, slashing motion across Matador's throat. As part of the single, fluid movement he released his grip on the small body so that it thudded to the ground, and the razor continued on its arc, unhindered until it met the soft leather of the saddlebag. The blade slit with fast ease, tumbling out a shower of bills which continued to flutter to the ground as Edge leapt upon the saddle, snatching a rifle from the boot on a nearby horse. Not a shot was fired at Edge as he heeled the horse forward, galloping towards the amazed bandits, who fell aside only in the last moment, began to scramble towards the fallen money, clawing each other aside in their greed.

And Edge fired only one round, as the hoofs of his mount lifted clear of the spread-eagled Luis Aviles. He wasn't sure, but he thought that just as the rifle exploded into sound, sending death into the old man's heart, the sun blackened, cracked flesh of Luis' face formed into a smile of thanks for this release from his agony. Then Edge reined the horse into a wide circle, drawing out of range to make his turn towards the south. But it was a manoeuvre for which there was no need. The bandits were too intent upon scooping up the money to spare time on Edge. And the bills in most demand were those stained by the blood still pumping from the gaping throat wound of the dead El Matador. 'I guess that must be what they call "Blood money",' Edge said as he galloped away, southwards.

CHAPTER SEVENTEEN

BUT Edge did not ride directly for the town of Montijo. As soon as he knew he would be lost from the sight of the bandits he swung in a wide circle and headed back towards them from a different direction. He rode the big white stallion at a slow walk, hid behind an outcrop of rock when he spotted a dust cloud to the north, waited until it had settled and the black specks of the riders had disappeared into the heat mirage before spurring his mount forward, faster than before but still not at a full gallop.

The buzzards lifted their cumbersome, satiated bodies into the still air while Edge was still many yards distant and when he rode up he saw they had dined well. El Matador was almost headless from the savagery of their tearing bills and they had excavated a great hole in the chest of Luis Aviles. Edge looked at the bodies impassively, nodded as he stooped over that of the old man, noting that he smelled worse in death than he had in life. He spent perhaps a full minute endeavouring to force the metal ring off the old man's finger, but it had obviously been worn for many years, refused to slide over the knob of the knuckle. Edge cursed softly, drew his razor and chopped off the finger neatly just beneath the ring. The ornament slid from the dead flesh easily now, its path greased by blood.

He looked at it through narrowed eyes, saw it was in the form of a short snake, the crudely carved head lapping over the tail to form a complete circle. The design meant nothing to Edge, but the old man had considered it important, so he wiped it free of blood. The only finger it would fit was the little one and this is where Edge wore it as he crossed to the body of El Matador, stopped and drew the two Colts, checked they had a full load before slipping them into his own holsters.

Then he remounted and set off southwards again, not looking

over his shoulder as a great flapping of wings told him of the return of the scavengers. The white stallion was strong and willing, experienced in the long, tough rides which are a part of bandit life. He carried his new rider into Montijo just as afternoon was lengthening into evening, the appearance of the big horse with its tall, hard-faced rider giving rise to many curious and suspicious glances. For the town was deep into Mexico, near the boundary between the Sonora and Sinaloa regions, far beyond the area where Americans normally ventured.

It was quite a large town, dependent for industry upon a sawmill and a silver mine, but inhabited mostly by peons who worked in the cane fields spread out to the south and east. There was little sign of activity on the fringe of the town, but as Edge rode down one of the two parallel main streets he could see lights and hear music and singing ahead. He ignored all who turned their suspicious eyes upon him, his own hooded and watching for signs of danger. But then he reined in his horse as a small boy of some ten years ran out in front of him, grinned at him with broken teeth.

'You an Americano?' the waif asked.

Edge looked at his dirt-streaked face, his tattered shirt and pants, guessing the boy's intention. He nodded and the grin broadened.

'I have a sister, señor,' he said and cupped his hands over his narrow chest, brought them forward in an explanatory movement. 'Very big here señor. She like Americanos. Very good with the love, señor.'

Edge injected some warmth into his expression, nodded along the street. 'What's going on.'

'Fiesta, señor. It is the mayor's birthday. He not a very good mayor, but everybody like him on his birthday 'cause he makes it a time for fiesta. Many girls in the cantina, señor. But expensive and not big here, like my sister.' Again the gesture with the hands.

Edge dipped into his pants pocket and brought out one of the dollars Gail had given him back in Peaceville. He dropped it to the feet of the boy who snatched it up with a filthy hand, suddenly wealthy by Mexican peon standards.

'Esteban!' a shrewish voice called from the shadow of a

108

building and the boy suddenly laughed and bolted for the opposite side of the street.

The woman came out into the open to give chase for the dollar and Edge grinned. She was big there. Also everywhere else and Edge heeled his horse into motion as the two hundred and fifty pound woman waddled in the wake of her agile young brother.

Both streets emerged into a plaza and exited on the far side, and here was the centre of the activities. Light, from torches and oil lamps, shone down upon a raised platform upon which a group of six guitar players provided music for fifty or more dancing couples. The plaza was fringed by ten cantinas from some of which emitted competing music, from others merely the shouts and screams of men and women making merry to honour the birthday of the mayor. Drunken figures of both sexes emerged from the swinging doors of the bars to either go into another cantina or join the dancers in the plaza. Grinning, dirty-faced youngsters who might have been cast in the same mold as Esteban, lit and threw firecrackers into the throng, bolting for safety whenever anybody threatened to give chase.

Here, the appearance of a stranger, whether he be a foreigner or Mexican, caused no reaction. Minds, made dull or benevolent by countless draughts of mezcal, tequila and pulque, considered that all was right in the world and wanted nothing more than to be allowed to continue with the merry-making. Edge eyed the scene impassively as he tied his horse to the rail fronting the Montijo Hotel, the big white animal looking incongruous among the mangy burros who shared the tether. But those who were most drunk in the throng probably considered the horse a figment of their imagination. Others cared nothing for the sight. Still more noted the expression on Edge's mean face and knew it would be unwise to question him.

Edge went into the cantina immediately adjacent to the hotel, found the tables packed with drinking men and women, many of them joining in with the song which a pretty young girl was wailing out from one end of the bar, accompanied by a leering young man on a guitar. Edge went to the other end of the bar, which was acting as a support for a line of swaying peons. One of the two sweating barmen came wearily towards

Edge, face set in a questioning stare.

'Señor?'

'Beer.'

The barman picked up a dirty glass, smashed the top from a bottle of beer and half poured it, muttered the price in pesos. Edge slapped a dollar bill on the bartop without attempting to touch the drink. A greasy hand covered the dollar and Edge brought the heel of his palm down on top. The barman looked up, fear leaping into his eyes, and found Edge grinning at him. He used his free hand to point at the ring on his little finger.

'That ought to mean something to someone in this town,' he said softly. 'The dollar's yours. If some guy don't come to see me at the hotel next door before midnight, I come back for my dollar. I also take something else.'

'Señor?' The man's eyes were wide.

'I ain't hearing so good with one ear,' Edge said, still grinning. 'Your's look healthy enough.'

The man swallowed hard and looked down at the hand which had trapped his, examined the ring.

'I do not know, señor,' he said.

'You better,' Edge told him and released his hand, turned from the bar and headed for the door. 'Name's Edge.'

The peon who had been standing next to him grasped the untouched beer and lifted it, tipped it down his throat.

'One tough, *hombre*,' he said to the barman. 'I think he mean it.'

'I *know* he means it,' the barman muttered as he watched the doors swinging behind the departing Edge.

The tall American unhitched his horse and led him off the plaza, found a livery stable in charge of a sleeping hostler. A boot in the ribs woke him and the sight of a dollar bill got him working. He promised Edge that even if El Presidente himself were to visit Montijo, the royal horse would receive no better treatment. Edge nodded his satisfaction and returned to the plaza, entered the hotel. The clerk announced he was fully booked, but a show of five dollars backed up by a narrow-eyed expression of determination enabled him to offer a single at the rear of the building, away from the noise of the fiesta. Edge had left his gear at the stable, and carried only the Spencer repeater he had stolen from one of El Matador's men. He signed the register and made the clerk repeat his name three times.

'I'm expecting company,' he said. 'Unless somebody comes in and asks for me, I don't want to be disturbed.'

'Certainly señor,' the clerk said, nervously, afraid of this tall, lean man with the evil face, knowing he would rather do without the five dollars than have the American in the hotel.

Edge started up the stairs with the rifle his only baggage, his lips pursed as if to whistle, but releasing no sound. He had been given room twenty-three and as he used the key on the lock a church bell tolled six times, far off and melancholy. He guessed it signified the time and wondered if he would have to wait the full six hours until deadline. He hoped not, especially when he lit the spluttering, foul-smelling kerosene lamp and looked at the room. It was little bigger than a closet, furnished with a narrow bed and a dresser with no mirror and two of its three drawers missing. There was one small window which looked out on to the blank face of the building behind the hotel. The floor was bare boards and as Edge crossed to the window two large cockroaches scuttled for the cover of the bureau. When Edge punched the blanket covered mattress a cloud of dust lifted, raising with it the stink of a hundred bodies which had rested there since the bedcover had last been washed or aired.

Edge grimaced and dragged the whole lot on to the floor, sending more cockroaches scuttling. Then he blew out the lamp and lay on the bare springs, which creaked with his weight. He used his hat for a pillow and did not close his eyes as he relaxed, content that he could see both the square of the moonlit window and the strip of light at the foot of the door. The sounds from the plaza came to him as a muted hum, only occasionally pierced by a loud shriek or burst of laughter. But he had gone too long without proper sleep and the distant, hypnotic sounds of the festivities, aided by the comforting feel of the rifle in his two hands, nudged Edge into a doze, pushed him down the slope into exhausted slumber.

'Señor, move one muscle and death will be your reward.'

Edge's eyes snapped open and he looked up at the trapdoor

in the ceiling he had not noticed before, saw it open to the sky, moonlight glinting on two revolver barrels.

'That ain't no kind of a deal,' he said and rolled off the bed, came up short and dropped his rifle as the door burst open to show another man holding two pistols on him.

'I am the guarantee, señor,' the second man announced.

'It's a deal,' Edge said, and froze.

CHAPTER EIGHTEEN

THE one who dropped lightly from the trapdoor in the ceiling was young – no more than twenty – with an innocent-looking, clean-shaven face in which soft brown eyes and a gentle mouth line suggested he was unused to the way of the gun. But the easy way he handled the two double trigger Tranter revolvers spoke of many years of experience. He was not a peon, for he was smartly turned out in a white shirt and grey pants and wore an expensive gunbelt with heavily ornamented buckle and holsters.

'I am Ramon Armendariz,' he introduced, stretching a foot to slide Edge's rifle under the bed. 'This is my uncle, Manuel Armendariz. We are the son and brother of the mayor of Montijo.'

He spoke excellent English, in the manner of one proud to air his knowledge.

'Two guys who like the first citizen every day of the year,' Edge answered.

The older man gave a short laugh. 'Señor Edge, even the mayor's mother does not like the mayor. She least of all, perhaps, because she can recall the pain she suffered in bringing such an animal into the world.'

Edge looked at him and could detect a vague family resemblance. Manuel was at least seventy, smaller by six inches than his nephew and wearing a full set of moustachio and beard, stained as white as his hair by the passing years. His eyes, too, were of a soft brown colouring, but shone with the bitterness of a harsh life instead of the anticipation of youth. His pistols were Colts.

'You must excuse our mode of entry,' Ramon said, smiling. 'But we heard that the manner of your approach lacked finesse. It suggested to us a man over-anxious to find that which he is seeking. Such a man can be dangerous.'

Edge grinned. 'I was sleeping like a baby.'

Ramon continued to smile. 'A baby with a lethal rattle in his hands,' he said, waving one of the Tranters towards the rifle.

'I cut my teeth on one like it,' Edge answered with a shrug.

'Did not we all,' Manuel said philosophically. 'We have all lived through violent times.'

'And now we are wasting time,' Ramon put in, dropping the smile. 'You have a ring, señor?'

'It means something to you?'

'How will I know until I see it?'

Edge brought his hands together, slid the ring from his finger and held it out. Ramon had to holster one of his revolvers to take the ring and as he did so, looking down at his side, Edge moved. He went on to the balls of his feet and side-stepped, spinning Ramon around and drawing a gun as his arm encircled the young man's throat. One of El Matador's Colts thudded into Ramon's back. Uncle and nephew looked across the room in horror as they realised they were facing each other with guns levelled.

'Drop them,' Edge demanded. 'Or after the fiesta Montijo will have a funeral.'

The younger man stiffened and Edge knew he was prepared to take his chances. But Manuel was much older and considerably more wise. He sighed and his revolvers clattered to the floor.

'You are too young to die, Ramon,' he said softly. 'And I am too old to want to.'

The fight went out of Ramon and his gun fell to the floor. Edge let go of his throat and used his free hand to hook the second gun from the young man's holster, let it fall. He pushed Ramon away from him, slid his own Colt back into its holster, grinned at the men's surprise.

'I didn't bring the mayor a present for his birthday,' he said. 'Instead, I give him the lives of two of his relations. It may not be much, but it's all I have at the moment.'

'It is not a trick, señor?' Manuel asked.

'You already told me I don't have any finesse,' Edge

answered. 'Look at the ring and tell me what it means to you.'

Ramon had to ignite the lamp for Manuel to find the fallen ring, and when he did retrieve it the old man carried it close to the light, bent his head close to examine it.

'What made you interested?' Edge asked, sitting on the bare springs of the bed, reaching below and picking up his rifle. He placed the weapon across his thighs, pointing at nothing.

Ramon leaned against the dresser. 'I am not,' he answered. 'My uncle, he became excited when he heard the story of your ring. He asked me to come to help him. Some help.'

Edge grinned. 'Luck of the draw.'

'My eyes are not so good as they once were,' Manuel said, and held out the ring. 'Here, Ramon. Tell me what is carved in the metal.'

The younger man crossed the room, took the ring and held it to the light, twisting and turning it, his face showing an expression of disgust for its tawdriness.

'It is worthless,' he said. 'Metal junk. A trinket, that's all.'

'The design!' Manuel said with harshness, licking his lips so that they shone through his white whiskers.

'A snake,' Ramon said with a shrug. 'Too badly formed to identify. A jararaca, maybe. Or perhaps a cascabel. I do not know.'

Now the old man's eyes shone, as well. He shook his head. 'It does not matter.' He looked at Edge. 'Where did you get the ring, señor?'

'My business.'

This did not discourage Manuel. 'From an old man, perhaps? Old like me? A Mexican?'

'Close enough.'

Manuel nodded his satisfaction. 'There is a story, señor. Of many bandits who stole much money from the army of the United States. Long ago. Many of the bandits were killed and only three were left when they arrived at Montijo.'

Ramon was suddenly interested, looking from his uncle, to Edge, to the ring. The last was suddenly no longer worthless.

'I heard something like that,' Edge allowed evenly.

Again the nod. 'In Montijo one of the bandits was killed. The other two captured. The money was never recovered. The two survivors went to prison. And soon the story died, for the sentences were long and few can survive long terms in the prisons of Mexico. But later, the story re-emerged as something of a legend and there were many romantic tales attached to the legend. One such was that when the three men were captured – one being killed, as I said – each wore a ring and these rings provided the clue to the hiding place of the stolen money.'

'How much money?' Ramon asked with a breathless tone.

Manuel's tongue flicked out once more and his voice was soft. 'The legend has it, ten thousand, American.'

Both Mexicans eyed Edge for confirmation.

'Close enough,' Edge said.

Ramon gasped. Manuel sighed.

'Much money,' the young man said. 'Not so much when split three ways.'

Edge now took hold of his rifle, but the muzzle continued to point at a blank wall.

'I ain't greedy,' he said. 'I came south to get back two and a half thousand that was stole from me. I had it and then had to let it go again. I'll be happy with something near eight hundred dollars profit from the trip.'

Manuel nodded, tugged at the shirt sleeve of his nephew. 'This is not Mexico City, Ramon,' he said sagely. 'To have something more than three thousand three hundred American dollars in Montijo, makes a man very rich indeed.'

Ramon considered this point for several moments and finally nodded his assent. But, in the spluttering oil lamp, Edge saw that the young man's greed had not diminished: merely retreated behind a thin veneer of pretense.

'We don't know where the money is hid yet,' Edge pointed out.

'The ring?' Manuel requested, extending his hand.

Ramon put it in his palm.

'What did you say the design represents?'

Ramon shrugged. 'A snake.'

Manuel smiled. 'You are perhaps too young to have sampled the delights at the southern end of Montijo,' he said softly. 'Or perhaps you are so handsome that you have not found the need to pay for your pleasures.'

For several moments the younger man continued to look at the ring with dull eyes, his smooth face creased by a deep frown of perplexity. But abruptly his features lit up.

'The bordello!' he exclaimed with excitement. 'I have been there. *El Serpiente*. The Snake.'

Edge sighed. 'With Luis, a bordello figures,' he muttered. 'Let's go.'

CHAPTER NINETEEN

ALTHOUGH the plaza of Montijo provided the centre of the fiesta it was not the only focal point of celebrations to mark the mayor's birthday. Just as Edge had been approached by Esteban as he rode in from the north, so other young pimps shouted offers as the three men passed through the southern end of town. They went on foot, having stopped off at the livery stable for Edge to collect his horse. Ramon had been suspicious of this, his uncle appearing to accept Edge's explanation of a pressing engagement out of town after he had collected his share of the money. But Edge had allowed the men to retrieve their weapons and the confidence of the revolvers convinced the younger man that he was capable of taking counter measures against an attempted double-cross: despite the speed of action the American had already exhibited to such effect.

All three ignored the offers, not bothering to reply to them and the young brothers of allegedly beautiful sisters did not press. For there was about the trio a latent menace that deterred interference with their determined progess. Edge sauntered along, leading the big white stallion by the bridle, flanked on the left by the strutting Ramon and on the right by the purposeful Manuel.

'There it is, señor,' Manuel said at length and Edge looked ahead with hooded eyes.

They were clear of the main town now and the street had become more uneven with the texture of an uncared-for trail. There was more space between the buildings on each side and most of them were small shacks, obviously the homes of the poorest of peons. But one was much larger than the rest, long and low, several yards deep, covering enough ground to allow for many rooms throughout the single storey of the structure. There was no light out here except that provided by the moon, but this pale luminescence was sufficient for the faded white lettering along the front of the building to be read: EL SERPIENTE.

Edge's narrowed eyes examined the side and front of the building as the trio drew level with it, saw that the windows were boarded up, the doors tightly closed, emitting no light.

'When were you last here?' Edge asked of Manuel.

The old man grinned. 'I am not too old to be lacking in all my faculties, señor,' he said. 'Last week I gave a good account of myself. It is not closed. The windows are shuttered to discourage prying eyes. *El Serpiente* only provide exhibition for money.'

Edge grunted and saw the bordello was indeed in business, for several burros were hitched to a rail at the far side of the building. He went to tether his horse and the two Mexicans waited for him to return before Manuel thudded a fist against the heavy doors.

'Do not break it down,' a shrewish female voice called in Spanish. 'The girls are here all night. All day, too, if you have the strength and the money.'

A heavy bolt was slid and the doors thrown open. Edge blinked in the sudden light, looked over the shoulder of a fat, elderly woman into a crudely decorated and sparsely furnished entrance hallway. He saw, in the light of ceiling-hung oil lamps, a number of women and girls lounging on sagging and burst sofas, seeking the newcomers with weary-eyed gazes.

'Ah,' the fat woman exclaimed with delight. 'Manuel and Ramon Armendariz. *El Serpiente* is honoured to entertain two members at once of our illustrious mayor's family.'

She punctuated her mocking welcome with a moist belch at which she and the two Mexicans laughed rowdily.

'I will tell my father you will not vote for him at the next election,' Ramon said with good humour.

'And get me closed up, or even shot?' the fat madam said with a pretense of horror. 'Come in, come in. Everything in my house is yours.'

Then she saw Edge, examined his height and build, the mean set of his features.

'Americano?' she whispered.

119

Manuel nodded and the woman smiled. 'He has much money, many dollars, to spend here?'

'And speaks much Spanish to ensure he is not cheated, señora,' Edge put in.

His knowledge surprised the woman. 'It is señorita, señor,' she corrected and grinned. 'I have seen too many faces of men in this business to ever choose to marry one.'

Edge looked over her shoulder again, at the selection of prostitutes arrayed for selection. They were of all shapes and sizes, ages and colorations, their bodies outlined by tight-fitting shifts falling from neck to ankles. But they had in common an expression of bitter acceptance of the life they had chosen, a look in their eyes which was almost animal in cast.

'I guess I've seen too many women like this to consider marriage myself,' he said.

The madam smiled and stood back, ushering the newcomers inside. 'That is good,' she said. 'Married men are bad customers. They come only as long as their wives do not find out. And wives are quick to know.'

Once inside the house, the doors were quickly slammed closed and Edge cast sidelong glances at the two Mexicans, saw that the memories of past visits were crowding into their minds. There had been no plan of campaign discussed as the trio set out for the bordello and now they were inside it, the Mexicans were obviously concerning themselves with a more urgent need than ten thousand dollars.

Edge himself had done no forward planning, had chosen to wait to see the set up before deciding how to go about locating the cache.

'Girls,' the madam said and the prostitutes rose wearily and pirouetted with a complete lack of grace.

As they turned Edge saw that each had a number sewn to the back of her shift and his eyes narrowed as he saw the numerals, his mind formulating the outline of his first attempt to find the money.

'Rosita for me,' Ramon said.

'And I'll take Margarita,' his uncle decided.

One girl, young and slim, stepped towards Manuel while another of almost forty with broad hips and large breasts approached Ramon. They were numbers ten and eight respectively. Many of the numbers between one and twenty-five were missing, their owners apparently already engaged with clients of the house.

'We number the girls for the benefit of Americanos not familiar with our language,' the madam explained to Edge. 'I can recommend numbers twelve and twenty-one, señor. Both are new. Not virgins, you understand, but almost.'

The two designated smiled beguilingly at Edge as the others glowered.

'I'll take one,' the tall American decided, his hooded eyes falling upon a thin girl who was very young and quite plain, with a narrow, small breasted body.

When the girl smiled at being chosen she showed a row of broken, much stained teeth.

The madam smiled. 'She is only twelve. We do not get many Americanos in Montijo, but when we do, they all choose the youngest. Maria is young in years, but experienced in the ways of love. Payment before.'

The woman held out her hand and was rewarded with pesos from the Mexicans, a dollar from Edge's fast-dwindling supply.

'The girls will show you the way,' she said, nodding to a door at the rear of the lobby as the unselected girls resumed their seats. 'If your partners please, I ask that you give them no money. I will collect it when you leave and put it in the bank for them.'

Everybody in the room knew she was lying, but nobody made a comment. Ramon and Manuel moved towards the door with their girls and Edge followed with the young Maria. The door gave on to a corridor badly lit in comparison with the lobby. As they moved down it, Edge saw that doors on each side were numbered with crudely painted numerals and from behind some of them came sounds of released passion. He formed his lips into a line of satisfaction when Margarita halted outside a door marked ten, opened it and stood aside for Ramon to enter. Then, further along, door eight was opened by Rosita who ushered Manuel inside.

'We will stay all night,' Manuel said in English. 'Until it becomes quiet and all are asleep.'

Edge nodded and went in the wake of Maria, following her to the very end of the corridor, where she opened the door numbered one, went in ahead of her client. The room was at the side of the building and Edge could hear the restless movements of the burros and his horse just beyond the boarded up window. This was something he had not planned for, but it fitted well with what he had in mind and his expression was almost one of smugness as he surveyed the room. It was little more than a narrow alcove, wide enough for a bed with a strip of bare floorboards beside it. On a shelf attached to the wall above the head of the bed was an array of feminine accoutrements. There was nothing else in the room.

But this did not cause Edge any concern. It was only his first attempt and he was prepared to fail. His thinking was that a single snake formed the design of the ring. Any reasonable number could have been incorporated, but had not been. Thus, one snake could indicate girl number one or room number one at *El Serpiente*. And, Edge thought, if he was in the right place, the money would not be on open display.

So he looked at the girl as she lit the stub of a candle, placed it in the centre of a dish upon the shelf.

'You require anything special, señor?' she asked dully, unbuttoning the top of her shift.

'Straight,' Edge said.

The girl's smile was a genuine one, of relief, then became hidden as she grasped the neck of the garment and pulled it up over her head. She was completely nude underneath, her body thinner than it appeared when covered, protruding bones giving it an ugly, angular appearance. Edge reached her in two short strides, drawing his right hand gun.

'You need some beauty sleep, honey,' he said in English and rapped her hard on the head with the gun butt, caught her body as it went limp.

He arranged her gently upon the bed, removing the shift from around her head so that she would not suffocate. He draped the garment carefully over her emaciated leanness and went to the door, looking for a lock. There was none and he cursed softly, moved to the shelf above the bed. He found a hairbrush and used his razor to slash away the matted bristles, then took hold of the candle and held it low, began to examine the dirt-streaked, dust covered floorboards. He found one which was loose and prised it up with his knife, had soon laid bare the earth beneath the strip of room beside the bed.

Using the bristleless brush as a shovel, he began to dig.

CHAPTER TWENTY

THE atmosphere in the tiny room was fetid and Edge sweated freely as he scooped up the earth with his makeshift shovel. There was no sign on the surface of the earth beneath the floorboards to indicate where, many years in the past, Luis Aviles and his two fellow bandits might have dug to bury their ten thousand ill-gotten dollars. So the tall man had to delve at random, going two feet down in each place before moving on to another. His expression of grim determination did not alter with each disappointment, and his concentration upon the task was never broken. Even when the candle exhausted its tallow and the flame spluttered out in the pool of liquid wax, he did not stop, knowing that the money would have been placed into a container before it was consigned to its grave: that the hairbrush would clash with some solid object to mark the end of his labour.

He had been working for upwards of an hour, so intent upon the task that he had forgotten about the unconscious Maria, could not even hear her regular breathing against the scraping of the hairbrush. Thus she came out of it without Edge being aware of the fact, and he did not see her fear-filled eyes surveying his back as he worked in a corner of the room; was ignorant of her slow, careful movement as she inched down the bed, placed her feet upon the floor and drew her naked body erect. The door latch gave the faintest squeak as she turned the handle, froze her to the spot, her body trembling from head to foot. As she pulled the door open the hinges gave an even lower creak, and she went out sideways, eyes fastened upon the impassive back of the intent American.

But this creak came simultaneously with a thud of the brush hitting wood and Edge went into a fast bout of furious digging and scraping. He was unaware of the door left ajar, of the low moan that escaped from the throat of Maria. Not until the door crashed open, smashing back against the wall and a flame touched a wick, burst into brightness, did Edge spin round on his haunches, go for his gun. Then he stayed his hand.

'Señor, you spent too long with such an inept girl, and you were too quiet.'

The speaker was Manuel, who levelled a Colt at Edge. Beside him, also holding a revolver in his right hand while his left raised an oil lamp was Ramon. Both were in their underwear and may have appeared ridiculous under other circumstances. At their feet lay the naked, unfortunate Maria, victim of yet another gun butt to her head.

'Please continue with the work of a rabbit, señor,' Manuel urged, waving the revolver, not attempting to enter the tiny room. 'We are most interested in what your burrowing will uncover.'

'You don't trust me, amigos,' Edge said.

'We do not trust our own mothers, señor,' came the reply.

Edge grinned coldly and returned to his work, light from Ramon's lamp spilling into the room and down the hole. He could see a narrow section of rotten wood which gave off an evil smell of mildewed decay as he continued to scrape earth from it.

'We decided, señor,' Manuel said in a conversational tone, 'that while a man could be rich in Montijo with over three thousand dollars, with five thousand he could be richer.'

'Logical, Mexican thinking,' Edge muttered, scraping away enough earth to reveal the top of what seemed to be a bullion box, some two feet by one.

'You will work a little faster, señor,' Manuel encouraged when Edge halted to examine his find.

There was an iron handle at one end and when he leaned into the hole to tug upon it the bolt securing one side ripped from the rotten wood. But the other bolt held and the lid came up with a dull creak of hinges rusted by time. As if she had been waiting for this as a signal Maria regained consciousness for the second time that night and on this occasion threw caution to the wind. Her thin mouth stretched wide and her scream was loud enough to reach into every room of the building, ripping sleep or lust from every mind in the place.

Edge leapt to his feet, going into a turn to bring him to face the door, saw Ramon and Manuel looking down at the screaming girl. The younger man's gun had followed the direction of his eyes so Edge shot Manuel first, the bullet entering his throat, gushing a fountain of bright red blood down upon the girl. Ramon squeezed the trigger of his revolver as a reflex action to the explosion of Edge's gun. His shot ended the scream of Maria by blasting away her jaw and as Ramon snapped up the Tranter and his eyes Edge's Colt spoke again. The bullet caught the handsome young man squarely between the eyes and a curtain of blood bathed his face as he fell with his uncle across the writhing body of the naked girl. The lamp fell from his lifeless fingers and sprayed the three of them with oil which immediately burst into flames. The screams and shouts which accompanied the thud of footfalls along the corridor were suddenly drowned by the shriek of utter horror and agonised pain as flames enveloped the flesh of the injured girl.

Edge looked down into the hole, the leaping flames providing ample light for him to see the contents of the rotted box. There was a gaping hole in one sid and there was a sole five dollar bill left intact to show the fortune it had once held. For the remainder had been reduced to chewed-up shreds of white and green, lining the box to provide a soft nest for six tiny white rats which cowered from the light while their ugly black mother stared upwards with blinded eyes and bared teeth.

'You dirty rats,' Edge snarled and emptied his revolver into the nest, hurled the exhausted weapon in after the shells.

Shouts from the blazing doorway drew Edge's attention and he unholstered the other Colt, fired in a rage through the leaping flames, heard a scream and saw the fat madam tumble into the room, blood spouting from her stomach, her clothes burning ferociously. He ignored her pleas for aid and turned to the boarded-up window, kicked once to shatter the glass, three times more to rip away the boards. Then he dived through the opening head first, leapt into the saddle of the white stallion and leaned forward to unhitch the reins.

He galloped fast towards the south, then swung west, finally north to take him in a wide sweep around the town. It was easy to keep track of his direction for he was able to take as his bearing the leaping flames of the *El Serpiente* bordello as the fire took hold of the entire building. He cast one final look over his shoulder, then heeled his mount into an even faster gallop northwards.

'Guess there's some real hot whores in the old town tonight,' he muttered.

NEL BESTSELLERS

NEL P.O. BOX 11, FALMOUTH, CORNWALL

Please send cheque or postal order. Allow 6p per book to cover postage and packing.

Name ....

Address..

....

Title ....
(APRIL)